Gulliver's Travels

To Lilliput & Brobdingnag

by

Jonathan Swift

CORE CLASSICS®

SERIES EDITOR MICHAEL J. MARSHALL

EDITED AND ABRIDGED BY MICHAEL J. MARSHALL

LIBRARY OF CONGRESS CATALOG CARD NUMBER: 97-75284

ISBN 1-890517-00-3 TRADE PAPERBACK

COPYRIGHT © 2001 CORE KNOWLEDGE FOUNDATION

ALL RIGHTS RESERVED · PRINTED IN CANADA

SECOND PRINTING

DESIGNED BY BILL WOMACK INCORPORATED

COVER ILLUSTRATION BY GB McINTOSH

TEXT ILLUSTRATIONS BY CHARLES E. BROCK 1894

CORE KNOWLEDGE FOUNDATION

801 EAST HIGH STREET

CHARLOTTESVILLE, VIRGINIA 22902

www.coreknowledge.org

Introduction

Introduction

WHEN *Gulliver's Travels* was written nearly 300 years ago, European explorers were making maps of all the world. But the Pacific Ocean, where some of the story takes place, was a mystery. Some geographers thought there must be an undiscovered continent somewhere in its lonely reaches. Explorers and sailors who came back from the Pacific wrote

vivid tales of their voyages and claimed to have seen
strange cultures and fantastic animals, such as unicorns,
griffins and giant eagles. Jonathan Swift presented his
book's hero, Gulliver, as such a traveler.

But *Gulliver's Travels* is not only about amazing
adventures. It is one of the great examples of satire. Satire
is a type of writing that tries to improve people's behavior
by showing how it is foolish. Satire tries to make us laugh
at our faults and want to change for the better.

Because some people who read the book might
think Swift meant to make fun of them, he tried to keep
his authorship secret. When he finished writing *Gulliver's
Travels*, he had a coachman drop it at the publisher's front
door in the dark of night. It did not have his name on it
anywhere. The publisher thought the story was left for
him by a ship's doctor named Lemuel Gulliver. Only later
did people learn the name of the true author.

Swift surely did have the people and politics of
his time in mind as he wrote, but he meant his satire to
be about human nature in any time or place. Pettiness,
pride and cruelty are faults we can see in ourselves.

Swift said he wanted to shake up readers. He
wondered if civilization, for all its clever inventions,

might not really be just a more complicated way for people to act like savages. He wanted us to see that we often do not use our ability to reason as we should. But we still have reasoning power, and we can use it to bring our bad behavior under control. Swift was discouraged about human nature, but hopeful for individual people.

Gulliver's name might make you think of the word gullible. As you get to know him, you'll have to decide if you think that is a good description. Gulliver seems certain of many facts. He fills his stories with details that make them seem realistic. But he sometimes seems fuzzy about knowing what is right and wrong. As you read, you should look for times when Gulliver's thinking does not make sense. Swift wanted you to exercise your ability to reason about good and bad, too.

E. D. HIRSCH JR.
CHARLOTTESVILLE, VIRGINIA

Gulliver's Travels

To Lilliput and Brobdingnag

PART I

A Voyage to Lilliput

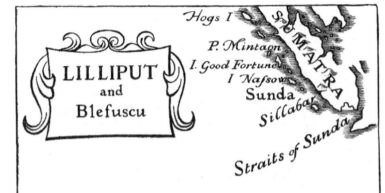

LILLIPUT
and
Blefuscu

Hogs I.

P. Mintagn
I. Good Fortune
I Nassow
Sunda
Sillabar

SUMATRA

Straits of Sunda

Blefuscu

Blefuscu

Mildendo LILLIPUT

Discovered, A.D. 1699

Dimens Land

Walker & Boutall sculpserunt

CHAPTER 1

Gulliver Is Shipwrecked and Captured

M Y FATHER HAD A SMALL ESTATE IN Nottinghamshire. I was the third of five sons. When I was 14 years old, my father sent me to Emmanuel College in Cambridge, where I studied for three years. But the cost of keeping me there was too great, so I was bound as an apprentice to Mr. James Bates, a highly respected surgeon in London, and I continued with him four years. My father now and then sent me small sums of money and I spent them on learning navigation and other parts of mathematics useful to those who travel, as I always believed it would be my fortune to do. When I left Mr. Bates, I went to **Leyden,** where I studied medicine, knowing it would be useful to me on long voyages.

LEYDEN
A city in Holland famous for its university.

Soon after my return from Leyden, Mr. Bates recommended me to be the ship's doctor on the *Swallow*, a ship on which I stayed three years and a half, making voyages to the **Levant** and other parts.

The last of these voyages was not very profitable and I grew weary of the sea. I intended to stay home with my wife and family, but after three years of little success in my practice, I accepted an offer to sail to the South Seas as the ship's doctor on the *Antelope*. We set sail from Bristol on May 4, 1699.

AUSTRALIA

Tasmania

VAN DIEMEN'S LAND
An earlier name for Tasmania, an island south of Australia.

At first we fared well, but as we sailed into the East Indies we were driven by a violent storm to the northwest of **Van Diemen's Land.** Twelve of our crew died from overwork and ill food; the rest were in a very weak condition. On the fifth of November, which is the beginning of summer in those parts, the weather was hazy. Seamen spied a rock near the ship, but the wind was so strong it drove us directly onto it. The ship immediately split. Six of the crew, of whom I was one, let down a boat into the sea and rowed clear of the ship and the rock. We rowed about three **leagues**, till we were able to work no longer. We trusted ourselves to the mercy of the waves. In about half an hour we were overturned by a sudden flurry from the north. What became of my companions in the boat, or those who escaped to the rock or were left in the ship, I cannot tell, but I assume that they all were lost.

For my own part, I swam and was pushed forward by wind and tide. I often let my legs drop and could

LEAGUE
A unit of distance ranging from 2.5 to 4.6 miles.

LEVANT
The countries on the eastern coast of the Mediterranean Sea, including Turkey, Syria, and Lebanon.

NOTTINGHAMSHIRE
A north-central county of England.

ENGLAND

EUROPE

Levant

MEDITERRANEAN SEA

Nottinghamshire

find no bottom. But when I was almost gone and able to struggle no longer, I found I could touch the bottom and the storm had died down. I walked nearly a mile before I got to the shore at about eight o'clock in the evening. I went on for nearly half a mile but could not discover any sign of houses or inhabitants. I was extremely tired. I lay down on the grass, which was very short and soft, where I slept sounder than I had ever slept in my life.

When I awoke it was just daylight. I attempted to rise, but was not able to stir. As I happened to lie on my back, I found my arms and legs were strongly fastened to the ground; and my hair, which was long and thick, was tied down. I also felt several slender cords across my body, from my armpits to my thighs. I could only look up. The sun began to grow hot and the light bothered my eyes. I heard noise about me, but I could see nothing except the sky.

In a little time I felt something alive moving on my left leg. Advancing gently forward over my breast, it came almost up to my chin. Bending my eyes downward as much as I could, I perceived it to be a human creature about six inches high, with a bow and arrow in his hands and a **quiver** on his back.

QUIVER
A portable case for arrows.

I WAS IN THE UTMOST ASTONISHMENT AND ROARED.

In the meantime I felt at least forty more of the same
kind following the first. I was in the utmost astonishment and roared so loud they all ran back in fright and
some of them, I was told later, were hurt by leaping from
my sides. However, they soon returned and one of them,
who ventured so far as to get a full sight of my face, lifting up his hands and eyes by way of admiration, cried
out in a shrill, clear voice, "Hekinah Degul!" The others

repeated the same words several times, but I did not know then what they meant.

I lay all this while in great uneasiness. Struggling to get loose, I broke the strings and wrenched out the pegs that fastened my left arm. At the same time, with a violent pull that gave me sharp pain, I loosened the strings that tied down my hair on the left side. I was just able to turn my head about two inches. But the creatures ran off a second time, before I could seize them. There was a great shout in a very shrill accent and when it was over, I heard one of them cry aloud, "Tolgo phonac!" In an instant I felt above a hundred arrows on my left hand, which pricked me like needles. They shot another flight into the air. Many fell on my body (though I did not feel them) and some on my face, which I immediately covered with my left hand.

When this shower of arrows was over, I was groaning with pain and I tried again to get loose. They let go another volley larger than the first and some of them attempted to stick spears in me, but by good luck I had a leather vest on, which they could not pierce. I thought it prudent to lie still. My intention was to continue so until night when, since my left hand was loose,

FROM THE NEWLY ERECTED STAGE, ONE OF THE INHABITANTS MADE
A LONG SPEECH, OF WHICH I UNDERSTOOD NOT ONE SYLLABLE.

I could easily free myself. As for the inhabitants, I believed I might match the greatest armies they could

bring against me if they were all of the same size as those that I saw.

When the people saw I was quiet, they shot no more arrows. But because the noise increased, I knew their numbers were greater. About four yards from me, near my right ear, I heard a knocking for more than an hour, like people at work. Turning my head that way, as far as the pegs and strings would permit me, I saw a stage erected about a foot and a half from the ground. It was capable of holding four of the inhabitants with two or three ladders to mount it. From there one of them, who seemed to be an important person, made a long speech, of which I understood not one syllable.

Before he began, he cried out three times, "Langro Dehul san!" (these words were later explained to me). Immediately about fifty of the inhabitants cut the strings that fastened the left side of my head, which gave me the liberty of turning it to the right and seeing the person speaking and his gestures. He appeared to be middle-aged and taller than the other three who stood with him, one of whom was a page who held up his train. He acted every part of an orator, and I could observe many gestures of threats and others of promises, pity and kindness.

I answered in few words, but in the most humble manner. Having not eaten a morsel for hours before I left the ship, I put my finger frequently on my mouth (even though it may not be good manners) to show I wanted food. The Hurgo (so they call a great lord) understood me very well. He came down from the stage and commanded that several ladders be placed at my sides, on which a hundred inhabitants mounted and walked towards my mouth with baskets full of meat. The Emperor had ordered these prepared when he first heard news of me. I observed there was the flesh of several animals, but could not tell them apart by taste. There were shoulders, legs and loins shaped like those of mutton, but smaller than the wings of a lark. I ate them two or three at a mouthful and took three loaves at a time that were about the big-ness of musket bullets. They brought food as fast as they could, showing astonishment at my appetite.

Then I made a sign I wanted a drink. They found that a small quantity would not satisfy me, and being ingenious people, they rolled one of their largest **hogsheads** toward my hand and beat out the top. I drank it all in a gulp, which I could easily do, for it held

HOGSHEAD
A large barrel containing from 63 to 140 gallons.

hardly half a pint. It tasted like a wine from **Burgundy**, but more delicious. They brought me a second hogshead, which I drank in the same manner. I made signs for more, but they had none to give me. When I had performed these wonders, they shouted for joy and danced on me, repeating "Hekinah Degul" several times. They made a sign for me to throw down the two hogsheads, but first warned the people below to stand out of the way. When they saw the vessels in the air, there was another shout of "Hekinah Degul!"

BURGUNDY
A region of France famous for its red wines.

I was often tempted when they were passing back and forth on my body to seize forty or fifty that came within reach and dash them against the ground. But I now considered myself bound by the laws of hospitality. They had treated me with so much expense and magnificence. I was amazed at the fearlessness of the tiny mortals who dared to climb and walk on me while I had one hand free, without trembling at the very sight of how huge I must appear to them.

After some time there appeared a person of high rank sent by his imperial majesty. He advanced up to my face with about a dozen attendants. He spoke for about ten minutes. He did not show any anger, but often pointed towards the capital city, where I must be taken. I answered in a few words, but to no purpose. I made a sign to show that I wanted my liberty. It seemed he understood me well enough. He shook his head and held his hand in a way to show I would be carried as a prisoner. He made other signs, too, to let me understand I would have meat and drink and good treatment.

I thought once more about attempting to break my bonds. But when I felt the stings from their arrows on my face and hands, which were all blistered and had many darts still sticking in them, and seeing that their numbers had increased, I let them know they could do with me as they pleased. Then the Hurgo and his attendants left with cheerful faces.

Soon I heard a shout and the cords on my left side were relaxed enough that I could turn on my right side. Before this, they dabbed my face and hands with ointment, very pleasant to smell, that took away the stings of their arrows. These circumstances caused me to fall asleep and I slept about eight hours. I later learned that the Emperor had ordered his doctors to put a sleeping powder in the hogsheads of wine.

It seems from the first moment I was discovered, the Emperor was informed. Consulting his advisors, he decided I should be tied as I was, given plenty of meat and drink, and a vehicle made to carry me to the city.

These people are excellent mathematicians and engineers, because of the encouragement of the Emperor, who is a patron of learning. He had several vehicles for hauling trees and other heavy weights. Five hundred carpenters set to work to build the biggest vehicle they ever had. It was a wood frame raised three inches off the ground, about seven feet long and four feet wide, moving on twenty-two wheels.

It was brought parallel to me as I lay. The difficulty was to raise me and place me in the vehicle. Eighty poles, each one foot high, were erected and very strong cords fastened to bandages were put under my neck, hands, body and legs. Nine hundred of the strongest men pulled up these cords by pulleys fastened on the poles. In less than three hours I was raised onto the vehicle and tied fast. All the time this happened I was asleep. Fifteen hundred of the Emperor's largest horses, each about four and a half inches high, pulled me toward the city, which was half a mile away.

FIFTEEN HUNDRED OF THE EMPEROR'S LARGEST HORSES, EACH ABOUT
FOUR AND A HALF INCHES HIGH, PULLED ME TOWARD THE CITY.

About four hours after we began our journey I
was awakened by a very ridiculous accident. The carriage was stopped to adjust something that was out of

order. Two or three curious young natives climbed up
very softly on my face and one of them, an officer of the
guards, put the sharp end of his **half-pike** up
my left nostril, which tickled my nose like a
straw and made me sneeze violently. It was
three weeks before I knew why I woke up so
suddenly.

HALF-PIKE
A spear-like
weapon.

We made a long march and rested at
night with five hundred guards on each side of
me, half with torches and half with bows and arrows
ready to shoot me if I stirred. At sunrise we continued
our march. By noon we arrived outside the city gates and
the Emperor and his court came out to meet us. His officers would not allow his Majesty to expose himself to
danger by climbing on my body.

The carriage stopped in front of an ancient temple, the biggest in the kingdom. A murder had happened
there some years before, so it was no longer sacred and
had been abandoned. In this building I was to lodge. Its
gate was about four feet high and two feet wide. I could
easily creep through. On each side of the gate was a
small window about six inches from the ground.
Through the left window the Emperor's blacksmith

THE CHAINS THAT HELD MY LEG WERE ABOUT TWO YARDS LONG.

passed ninety-one chains, which were locked to my left leg with thirty-six padlocks.

Opposite the temple, on the other side of the highway, was a turret at least five feet high. Here the Emperor climbed, with many of his lords, to have a chance to view me. I could not see them. More than a hundred thousand inhabitants came out of the town for the same purpose, and no fewer than ten thousand climbed up on my body, many times. But soon a proclamation was issued that forbade climbing on me on pain of death.

When the workmen saw that it was impossible for me to break loose, they cut the strings that bound me. I rose up in as sad a mood as I ever had in my life. The noise and astonishment of the people at seeing me stand up and walk cannot be expressed. The chains that held my leg were about two yards long and let me walk back and forth in a semicircle and creep in and lie at my full length in the temple.

CHAPTER 2

Gulliver Meets the Emperor of Lilliput

WHEN I LOOKED ABOUT ME, I CONFESS I never beheld a more delightful sight. The country appeared like a garden and the fields, which were generally forty feet square, resembled beds of flowers. These fields were mixed with woods and the tallest trees were about seven feet high. The town, on my left, looked like the painted scenes of a city in a theater.

The Emperor had already come down from the tower and advanced on horseback toward me. It nearly cost him some injury, because the animal, unused to the sight of me, who appeared like a mountain moved before him, reared up. But that Prince, being a good horseman, kept his seat until his attendants ran in and held the bridle while his Majesty dismounted. He surveyed me, but kept beyond the length of my chains.

He ordered his cooks to give me food and drink, which they pushed forward in vehicles until I could reach them. I soon emptied them all, twenty full of meat and ten with liquor. Each of the former gave me two or three good mouthfuls. I emptied the liquor of the ten vessels into one, drinking it off in a gulp.

The Empress and the young princes and princesses sat at some distance in chairs, but when the accident happened with the Emperor's horse, they got up and came near him. He is taller, by almost the width of my fingernail, than anyone in his court, which alone is enough to strike awe into his subjects. His features are strong and masculine, his bearing erect, his body well-proportioned, his movements graceful and his manners majestic. He was past his prime, being 28 years old, and had reigned for seven years in great happiness.

To see him more conveniently, I lay on my side, so that my face was parallel to his. He stood three yards off. I have held him in my hands many times since then. His clothes were very plain and simple, but he had on his head a light helmet of gold, adorned with jewels and a plume on the crest. He held his sword in his hand, to defend himself if I should break loose. It was almost three inches long. The **hilt** and **scabbard** were gold enriched with diamonds. His voice was shrill, but clear. I could hear it distinctly when I stood up. The ladies and courtiers were magnificently dressed. The spot where they stood seemed like a petticoat spread on the ground. His Imperial Majesty spoke to me and I answered, but neither of us could understand a syllable. Several of his priests and lawyers were commanded to address me; I spoke to them in the languages I knew a little of, which were Dutch, Latin, French, Spanish, and Italian, but all to no purpose.

HILT
The handle of a weapon.

SCABBARD
A sheath or container for a sword.

After two hours the court departed. I was left with a strong guard to prevent the rabble from crowding about me as near as they wanted to. Some of them had the rudeness to shoot arrows at me as I sat at the door of my house, and one very narrowly missed my left eye. The colonel ordered six of the ringleaders seized and bound.

SOME OF HIS SOLDIERS PUSHED THEM FORWARD
WITH THE BLUNT ENDS OF THEIR PIKES.

He could think of no punishment more fitting than to
deliver them to me. Some of his soldiers pushed them
forward with the blunt ends of their pikes. I took them
all in my right hand, put five in my coat pocket, and
looked at the sixth as if I meant to eat him alive. The
poor man squalled terribly. And the colonel and his offic-

ers were afraid when they saw me take out my penknife. But I soon put their fear to rest. I cut away the strings he was bound with and gently set him on the ground. Away he ran. I treated the rest the same way, taking them out of my pocket one by one. The soldiers and people were delighted with my mercifulness.

Towards night I got into my house, with some difficulty, where I lay on the ground. That continued for two weeks, during which time the Emperor ordered a bed to be made. Six hundred beds of their ordinary size were brought in my house. Then they were sewn together to make four layers and stacked. They were barely better than the hardness of the floor, which was smooth stone. In the same way, I was also provided sheets and blankets good enough for one like me who is used to hardships.

As news of my arrival spread through the kingdom, great numbers of rich, idle and curious people came to see me. The villages almost emptied and household affairs would have been neglected if his Imperial Majesty had not issued proclamations against it. He directed those who had already seen me to return home and not to come within fifty yards of my house without a license from the court. This raised considerable fees for officials.

In the meantime, the Emperor held many councils to debate what should be done with me. They feared that I might break loose and that feeding me would be expensive and cause a famine. They thought about starving me or shooting me in the face and hands with poison arrows. But they worried the stink from such a large corpse might cause a plague in the city that would probably spread through the whole kingdom. At one meeting several officers of the army came to the council chamber and told how I had treated the six criminals I just talked about. This made such a favorable impression that an Imperial Order was issued requiring all the villages within nine hundred yards of the city to deliver six beef cattle, forty sheep and other food, including bread and wine, for me to eat. His majesty paid for this from his treasury. His wealth comes chiefly from his own estates and he rarely puts taxes on his subjects. Six hundred people were hired as my servants and tents were built for them at each side of my door. Three hundred tailors were ordered to make a suit of clothes for me in the fashion of Lilliput. Six scholars were hired to teach me their language and, finally, the Emperor's horses and those of the guards were exercised in my sight so that they could get accustomed to me. In three weeks I made great progress learning their language. The Emperor often visited and helped the scholars teach me.

We began to talk together and the first words I learned were those to express my desire to be free, which I repeated every day on my knees. His answer was that this would take time and would not happen without the advice of his council. First I must swear a peace with him and his kingdom. He said I would be treated kindly. He advised me to earn the good will of his subjects through patience and good behavior.

He asked me not to be upset if he ordered his officers to search me for weapons, which must be very dangerous things if they matched the bulk of so huge a person. To satisfy him I said I was ready to strip and turn out my pockets. He replied that by the laws of his kingdom, I must be searched by two officers. He knew this could not be done without my consent and that he had such a good opinion of my generosity and justice that he trusted me with his officers in my hands.

Whatever they took from me would be returned when I left the country or paid for at a cost I set. I took up the two officers in my hands and put them first in my coat pockets and then into every other pocket except my two watch pockets and another secret pocket that I did not want searched. It had some little items of no importance to anyone but me. In one watch pocket was a silver watch and in the other a small amount of gold in a purse. These gentlemen, who had pen, ink and paper, made an exact inventory of everything they saw and what they had done. I later translated it into English and it follows.

In the right coat pocket of the Great Man Mountain, after a strict search, we found one piece of coarse cloth, large enough to be a rug for your Majesty's throne room. In the left pocket, we saw a huge silver chest which we were not able to lift. We desired that it be opened, and one of us stepped in, sinking up to his knees in some sort of white dust that flew up in our faces and **set us both sneezing** several times.

In his right coat pocket we found a bundle of white thin substances, folded one

They sneezed because this was a snuff box containing ground-up tobacco that was inhaled or placed next to the gums.

above the other about the bigness of three men, tied with a strong cable and marked with black figures. We believe them to be writings. Every letter is almost half as large as the palms of our hands. In the left pocket was some sort of machine with twenty poles sticking from it. We think the Man Mountain combs his head with it. We did not always bother to question him because we found it difficult to make him understand us.

In his right pants pocket was **a hollow iron tube**, about the length of a man, fastened to a large timber the size of a pillar, which we don't know what to make of. In the left pocket was another machine of the same kind. In a small pocket on the right side were several round flat pieces of white and red metal. Some of the white, which seemed to be silver, were so large and heavy we could hardly lift them. In the left pocket were two black pillars unusually shaped. Within each was a huge plate of steel. He took them out of their cases and told us that in his country he shaved his beard with one of them and cut his meat with the other.

The metal tube on a wooden pillar was a pistol.

Two pockets we could not enter. They were two large slits cut into the top of his pants, squeezed closed by the pressure of his body. The right one had a great silver chain hanging from it with a wonderful kind of machine at the end. It appeared to be a globe, half silver, half some transparent metal. On one side certain strange figures were drawn. We thought we could touch them but our fingers were stopped by that clear substance. He put this machine to our ear and it made a constant noise, like a water mill. We speculated that it is an unknown animal or the god he worships. We think the latter because he told us he seldom does anything without consulting it. He called it his oracle and said it pointed out the time for every action in his life. From the left slit he took out a net, big enough for a fisherman, that opened and shut like a purse. We found several pieces of yellow metal in it, which if they are real gold, must have immense value.

Having, in obedience to your Majesty's commands, carefully searched his pockets, we observed a belt around his waist from which hung a sword as long as five men and a pouch. The pouch had two compartments, each of which could hold three of your Majesty's subjects. In one part were globes of heavy metal, about as big as our heads, and the other part contained a heap of black powder.

IT APPEARED TO BE A GLOBE, HALF SILVER,
HALF SOME TRANSPARENT METAL.

This is an exact inventory of what we found on the body of the Man Mountain, who treated us courteously. Signed and sealed on the fourth day of the eighty-ninth moon of your Majesty's reign.

Clefren Frelock, Marsi Frelock

When this inventory was read to the Emperor, he asked me to give him several items. He first wanted my sword. Meanwhile he ordered three thousand of his best troops to surround me with their bows and arrows ready. But I did not notice. My eyes were fixed on his Majesty. He wanted me to draw my sword. I did so and immediately the troops gave a shout of terror. The sun was bright and the reflection dazzled their eyes as I waved the sword back and forth. His Majesty was less afraid than I expected. He asked me to return it to the scabbard and cast it to the ground as gently as I could, about six feet from the end of my chain.

Next he demanded one of my pistols. I took it out and, as well as I could, explained how it is used and loaded it just with powder. I cautioned the Emperor not to be afraid and then fired into the air. Hundreds fell down as if they had been struck dead. Even the Emperor, who stood his ground, could not recover himself for some time. I gave up my pistols, powder and bullets, begging him to keep the powder away from fire. The smallest spark could blow his palace into the air. I also gave up my watch, which the Emperor was very curious to see. He commanded two of his tallest guards to carry it on a pole on their shoulders. He was amazed at the continual noise it made and the motion of the minute hand. I then gave up my silver and copper money, my purse with nine pieces of gold, my knife and razor, my comb and silver snuff box, and my handkerchief and journal. My sword, pistols and powder were taken to his Majesty's warehouses, but the rest of my things were returned to me.

In the private pocket that escaped their search were a pair of spectacles and a small telescope that I feared might be lost or spoiled if I let them out of my possession.

CHAPTER 3

Amusements at
the Court of Lilliput

MY GENTLENESS AND GOOD BEHAVIOR so impressed the Emperor, his court, and the people in general that I began to hope of getting my liberty. I did everything I could to encourage that to happen. The natives gradually became less afraid of danger from me. I would sometimes lie down and let five or six of them dance on my hand. And at last boys and girls dared to play hide and seek in my hair. By now I had made good progress in understanding and speaking their language.

The Emperor one day decided to entertain me

with country shows. None impressed me so much as the rope-dancers, who performed on a slender thread stretched about two and a half feet above the ground. These performances are put on only by those who are candidates for high positions at court. They are trained in this art from an early age. When an important office is open, because of either death or disgrace, five or six candidates ask the Emperor for a chance to entertain the court with a rope dance. Whoever jumps the highest without falling wins the job. Often the chief ministers themselves are commanded to show their skill and convince the Emperor they have not lost their ability. Flimnap, the treasurer, can **cut a caper** on a straight rope at least an inch higher than any other lord in the empire. I have seen him do somersaults several times on a serving platter attached to the rope.

CUT A CAPER
To dance.

The performances often include fatal accidents. I myself have seen two or three candidates break a limb. The danger is greatest when the ministers are commanded to perform because they strain themselves so that hardly any has not fallen. I was told that a year or two before my arrival, Flimnap surely would have broken his neck if one of the Emperor's cushions, which was accidentally left on the ground, had not softened his fall.

There is another entertainment that is performed only for the Emperor and Empress on special occasions. The Emperor lays on a table three silk threads each six inches long. One is blue, one is red, and the third is green. These threads are prizes in a ceremony the Emperor performs in his throne room. He holds a stick in his hands and the candidates advance one by one, sometimes leaping over the stick and sometimes creeping under it. They go back and forth several times as the stick is raised or lowered. Whoever is the most agile at leaping and creeping gets the blue silk, the red silk goes to the next best, and the green to the third best. Very few people around the court are not adorned with these threads around their waists.

Blue, red and green are the colors of the three orders of the knighthood in England.

The horses of the army were no longer shy and would come up to my feet without being startled. Riders would jump them over my hand as I held it on the ground. One, on a large charger, jumped my shoe, which was indeed a huge leap.

I amused the Emperor one day in a very extraordinary manner. I asked him to order several sticks two feet high and about as thick as a cane. I took nine of these sticks and fixed them firmly in the ground in a square shape, two and a half feet wide. I took four other sticks and tied them, like rails, to the corners, and then fastened my handkerchief to the sticks that stood upright until it was as tight as the top of a drum. When I finished, I asked the Emperor to let a troop of his cavalry exercise on this plain. He approved and I took them up one by one, already mounted and armed, in my hands. They performed mock skirmishes, fired blunt arrows, and attacked and retreated. The rails kept them from falling off the stage.

The Emperor was so delighted he ordered this entertainment repeated for several days. Once I lifted him up to give the word of command. Even the Empress was persuaded to let me hold her where she could take full view of the performance. By good luck no accidents happened during these exercises. Only once a fiery horse pawing with his hoof tore a hole in my handkerchief and threw his rider. But I picked them up and, covering the hole, set the cavalry back down.

About three days before I was set free, a messenger arrived to tell his Majesty that some of his subjects, riding near where I was found, had seen a great black substance lying on the ground. It had wide, round edges, rising up in the middle as high as a man. It was not a living creature, as they thought at first. It did not move. Some of them walked around it several times and, climbing to the top and stomping on it, they found it was hollow. They thought it might be something belonging to the Man Mountain. If his Majesty wanted them to, they could bring it with only five horses.

I knew what they meant and was glad to get this news. My hat, which had been fastened to my head with a string and stuck on all the time I was swimming, fell off after I came to land. I had assumed I lost it at sea. I urged his Majesty to order it brought to me as soon as possible. The next day it arrived, but not in very good condition. They had drilled two holes in the brim, put hooks in the holes and dragged it for more than half a mile. But the ground there is smooth and level and the hat was less damaged than I expected.

Two days later, the Emperor ordered the part of his army that lives in the city to be on alert. He wanted

HE WANTED ME TO STAND LIKE A COLOSSUS,
WITH MY LEGS SPREAD AS FAR APART AS WAS COMFORTABLE.

me to stand like a **colossus**, with my legs spread as far apart as was comfortable. He then commanded his general to form the troops in close order and march them under me. This parade consisted of three thousand men on foot, twenty-four men across, and one thousand on horses, sixteen horses across, with drums beating, flags flying and pikes pointed forward. The Emperor had ordered everyone to mind good manners, but some young officers looked up. To tell the truth, my pants were so badly worn in places that some of them laughed out loud.

COLOSSUS
A huge statue such as the Colossus of Rhodes, one of the seven ancient wonders of the world, or the Statue of Liberty.

I had asked so often for my liberty that his Majesty finally mentioned the matter to his council. It was opposed by no one except Skyresh Bolgolam, admiral of the realm, who, without being provoked by me, chose to be my enemy. The council was in my favor and the Emperor agreed, but Skyresh Bolgolam was allowed to make up the rules under which I would be set free. He brought them to me himself and, after reading them to me, demanded that I swear agreement to them first in the manner of my own country and then according to their laws. Their method forced me to hold my right foot in my left hand, place the middle finger of my right hand on the top of my head and my thumb on the tip of my right ear. I translated the document as near as I was able.

Golbosto momaren evlame gurdilo shefin mully ully gue, mighty Emperor of Lilliput, delight and terror of the universe, whose dominions extend five thousand *blustrugs* (about 12 miles around) to the ends of the globe: Monarch of all monarchs; taller than the sons of men, whose feet press down to the center, and whose head strikes the sun; at whose nod the princes shake their knees; pleasant as the Spring; comfortable as the Summer; fruitful as the Autumn; dreadful as the Winter. His Majesty proposes these rules to the Man Mountain, who swears an oath he will observe them:

I. The Man Mountain shall not leave without permission.

II. He shall not come to our city without being ordered, and the city's inhabitants will have two hours' warning of his coming.

III. *The Man Mountain shall walk only on main roads and not lie down in meadows or corn fields.*

IV. *As he walks he shall take care not to trample our subjects, horses or carriages, nor take any subject in his hands without their consent.*

V. *If a message is extremely urgent, he shall carry in his pocket the messenger and his horse and return the messenger safely.*

VI. *He shall help us against our enemies on the Island of Blefuscu and do his best to destroy their fleet, which is preparing to attack us.*

VII. *The Man Mountain shall help our workmen raise large stones.*

VIII. *Man Mountain shall, in two moons' time, measure the boundary of our lands according to his own steps around our coast.*

Lastly, when he makes a solemn oath to follow these rules, he shall have daily food and drink, access to his Majesty, and other signs of favor.

HE COMMANDED ME TO RISE AND PROVE MYSELF A USEFUL
SERVANT AND DESERVING OF ALL THE FAVORS HE HAD GIVEN ME.

I swore with cheerfulness, even though some of
the rules were not as honorable as I would have wished.
My chains were immediately unlocked and I was free.
The Emperor himself attended the ceremony. I got down
by his feet to show my thankfulness. He commanded me
to rise and prove myself a useful servant and deserving
of all the favors he had given me.

CHAPTER 4

Mildendo,
the Capital of Lilliput,
and the Emperor's Palace

THE FIRST REQUEST I MADE ONCE I WAS FREE was to see Mildendo, the capital, which the Emperor easily granted. He told me to be careful not to hurt the people or their houses. The people were given notice of my intention to visit the town. The wall surrounding it is two and a half feet high and eleven inches wide, so that a coach can be driven safely around it, and has strong towers every ten feet. I stepped over the wall at the western gate and eased very

I WALKED WITH THE GREATEST CAUTION
TO AVOID TREADING ON ANY STRAGGLERS.

gently through the two main streets. I took off my coat for fear of damaging the roofs of the houses. I walked with the greatest caution to avoid treading on any stragglers, even though there were strict orders for all people to stay in their houses. The attic windows and housetops were crowded with spectators.

The city is an exact square, each side of the wall being five hundred feet long. The two main streets that cross and divide the city into four quarters are five feet wide. The lanes and alleys were too narrow for me to enter. I only viewed them as I passed. The town can hold five hundred thousand souls. Its houses are from three to five stories high.

The Emperor's Palace is in the center of the city, where the two great streets meet. It is enclosed by a wall two feet high and is twenty feet away from other buildings. I could easily view the Palace on every side. The outer courtyard is a square. In the center are the royal apartments, which I very much wanted to see. The buildings of the outer courtyard are five feet high and it was impossible for me to step over them without causing damage.

At the time, the Emperor wished for me to see the magnificence of his Palace, but I was not able to until three days later. I spent them cutting down some of the largest trees in the royal park with my knife and making them into two stools strong enough to bear my weight. When the people had been given notice again, I went to the Palace with my two stools. When I came to the outer courtyard, I stood on one stool, lifted the other one over the roof and gently set it down in the inner courtyard, which was about eight feet wide. Then I stepped over the buildings from one stool to the other and then picked up the first stool with a hooked stick. I lay down on my side, put my face up to the middle stories and discovered the most splendid rooms that can be imagined. I saw the Empress and the young princes and their attendants. Her Majesty smiled at me very graciously and put her hand out the window for me to kiss.

One morning, Reldresal, the secretary of private affairs, came to my house with one servant. He ordered his coach to wait and said he wanted an hour of my time. I offered to lie down, but he chose to let me hold him in my hand during our conversation.

He said I might not have been freed so soon if it were not for the situation facing the court. As flourishing as things might look to a foreigner, he said, two mighty

HER MAJESTY SMILED AT ME VERY GRACIOUSLY
AND PUT HER HAND OUT THE WINDOW FOR ME TO KISS.

evils threatened the country. One was violent political strife in the empire and the other was the danger of invasion by a powerful enemy.

For seventy moons, two parties had struggled, the Tramecksan and the Slamecksan, who were told apart by the high heels or low heels on their shoes. His Majesty determined to employ only low heels in his government. His heels are lower than anyone else's in his court. The hostility between the two parties runs so high that they will not eat, nor drink nor talk with each other.

"We figure the Tramecksan, the high heels, outnumber us," Reldresal said, "but we have power entirely on our side. However, we suspect the heir to the throne has a tendency towards the high heels. We can plainly see one of his heels is higher than the other and so he walks with a hobble.

"Along with this trouble, we are threatened with an invasion from the island of Blefuscu, the other great empire of the universe. As for what you say, that there are other kingdoms and states in the world, inhabited by human creatures as large as you are, our philosophers doubt that. They guess you dropped from the moon, or a star, because a hundred humans your size would soon eat up all the fruit and cattle in his Majesty's dominions. Besides, our histories, which go back six thousand moons, make no mention of other empires than Lilliput and Blefuscu.

HE BROKE IT THE ANCIENT WAY AND HAPPENED TO CUT HIS FINGER.

"These two mighty powers have been at war for thirty-six moons. It started this way. Everyone agrees that the primitive way to break an egg was on the **larger end**. Once when his Majesty's grandfather was a boy and was going to eat an egg, he broke it the ancient way and happened to cut his finger. So his father commanded all his subjects to break only the **smaller end** of

BIG- AND LITTLE-ENDERS
Swift is alluding to disputes between Protestants and Roman Catholics.

their eggs. The people have so highly resented this law that there have been six rebellions because of it. **One Emperor lost his life and another his crown.** These rebellions were constantly encouraged by the monarchs of Blefuscu, and when they are put down, the exiles always fled to that empire for refuge. In all, eleven thousand persons have chosen to die rather than break their eggs at the smaller end. Many hundred large volumes have been published on this controversy. But the books of the Big-Endians have been long forbidden. During these troubles the Emperors of Blefuscu have accused us of causing a split in religion, saying we sin against the teaching of the Brundecal. But the words of that book are these: All true believers shall break their eggs at the convenient end.

> Swift is alluding to the reigns of the English kings Charles I and James II.

"Meantime we have lost forty ships and many more small vessels, plus thirty thousand sailors and soldiers. The damage to the enemy is reckoned to be larger, but they have built a large fleet and are preparing to attack us. His Majesty commanded me to tell you this," Reldresal said.

I humbly asked him to let the Emperor know that it was not my business, as a foreigner, to interfere with the parties, but I was ready to risk my life to defend him and his country from all invaders.

CHAPTER 5

The Invasion of Lilliput and the Fire in the Palace

THE EMPIRE OF BLEFUSCU IS AN ISLAND northeast of Lilliput and separated from it by a channel eight hundred yards wide. I had not yet seen it and avoided appearing on that side of the coast for fear of being seen by the enemy's ships. They had no knowledge of me. I told his Majesty of a project I had formed of seizing the enemy's whole fleet. Our scouts assured us it lay at anchor ready to sail with the first fair wind. I consulted the most experienced seamen about the depth of the channel. In the middle, they said, at high tide it was seventy glumgluffs deep, which is about six feet, and the rest was fifty glumgluffs deep.

I walked to the coast across from Blefuscu, lay down behind a small hill and took out my pocket telescope to view the enemy's fleet. It consisted of fifty warships and a great number of transports. Then I went back to my house and ordered a large amount of strong cable and iron bars. The cable was as thick as twine and the bars about the size of knitting needles. I tripled strands of the twine together to make it stronger and likewise twisted bars of iron together in threes, bending the ends into hooks. I made fifty hooks and fifty cables. I went back to the coast, took off my coat, shoes and socks and walked into the sea about half an hour before high tide.

I waded as fast I could and swam in the middle until I could feel the bottom again. I arrived at the fleet in less than half an hour. The enemy was so frightened when they saw me they leaped from their ships and swam to shore, where at least thirty thousand souls gathered. I then fastened a hook to the prow of each ship and tied all the cords together. The enemy shot several thousand

I TOOK UP THE CORD AND EASILY PULLED FIFTY OF
THE ENEMY'S LARGEST WARSHIPS AFTER ME.

arrows while I was doing this, many of which stuck in my
hands and face and, besides stinging sharply, disturbed
my work. My greatest fear was for my eyes, which I would
have lost, if I had not had a pair of spectacles in a private
pocket. I fastened these as strongly as I could to my nose
and went on boldly with my work. The enemy's arrows
struck the glass, but had no effect. I now began to pull,

but no ship would stir. They were all held in place by their anchors. I therefore let go of the cords and boldly cut the cables to their anchors. I received more than two hundred shots in the face and hands doing this. Then I took up the cords and easily pulled fifty of the enemy's largest warships after me.

The Blefuscudians were astonished. They thought my plan was to let the ships drift or run into each other. But when they saw me pulling the whole fleet together, they gave a scream of despair that is impossible to describe. When I was out of danger, I stopped to pick the arrows out of my face and hands and rub on some ointment. I took off my spectacles and waited about an hour until the tide was low and waded on to Lilliput.

The Emperor and the whole court stood on the shore expectantly. They saw the ships move forward in a half moon shape, but could not see me, because I was up to my chest in the water. They were more upset when I was in the middle of the channel because I was in water up to my neck. The Emperor assumed I had drowned and the enemy's fleet was approaching in a hostile manner. But the water got shallower with every step and when I came within hearing I cried out loudly, "Long live the Emperor of Lilliput!" He welcomed me with all possible praises and made me a Nardac on the spot, which is their highest honor.

His Majesty wished I would bring all the rest of the enemy's ships to Lilliput too. So vast was his ambition that he seemed to think of nothing less than making all the Empire of Blefuscu into a province, of destroying the Big-Ender exiles, and forcing the Blefuscudian people to break the smaller ends of their eggs. That would make him the sole monarch of the whole world. I tried to turn him away from this plan. I protested I would never help bring free and brave people into slavery. When the issue was debated in council, the wisest ministers agreed with me.

This open stand of mine was so opposite to the schemes of his Majesty that he could never forgive me. From this time, his Majesty and a group of ministers who were secret enemies to me began to plot my destruction. So little do services to princes matter compared to things refused to them.

About three weeks after this, ambassadors from Blefuscu arrived with offers of peace. There were six ambassadors with about five hundred others, and their entry was very magnificent. When their treaty, which was very advantageous to our Emperor, was finished, they made a visit to me, having been told privately how much I had been their friend. They complimented my valor, invited me to their kingdom, and asked me to show them my tremendous strength.

When I had entertained their excellencies to their great satisfaction and surprise, I asked them to present my humble respects to their Emperor, whom I desired to visit before I returned to my own country. Thus, the next time I had the honor to see our Emperor, I asked his permission to visit the Blefuscudian monarch, which he granted me in a very cold manner. I could not guess the reason for this until it was whispered to me that Flimnap and Bolgolam had described my meeting with the ambassadors as a sign of disloyalty, which I am sure in my heart it was not. I began to get an idea of how courts and ministers are.

It was not long before I had the opportunity to do his Majesty what I thought was a most distinguished service. I was alarmed at midnight by the cries of many hundred people at my door. Being suddenly awakened, I was in a kind of terror. Several members of the court

THE AMBASSADORS FROM BLEFUSCU ARRIVED WITH OFFERS OF PEACE.

begged me to come immediately to the Palace, where her Imperial Majesty's apartment was on fire. It had been caused by the carelessness of a maid, who fell asleep while reading a **romance**. I got up in an instant and, with the aid of moonlight, got to the Palace without trampling any peo-

ROMANCE
A tale of amazing heroes and unbelievable events.

ple. People supplied me with buckets, about the size of a thimble, as fast as they could but the flame was so violent, they did little good. I might have stifled it with my coat, but in my haste I came with only my leather vest. The case seemed desperate. The magnificent Palace would have been burnt to the ground if I had not suddenly thought of something to do. I had drunk a lot of a delicious wine the evening before and by the best luck in the world, I had not discharged any of it yet. I relieved myself in such a quantity and so well to the proper places that in three minutes the fire was entirely put out. The rest of that noble building, which had taken so many years to build, was preserved from destruction.

It was now daylight and I returned to my house, without waiting to congratulate the Emperor, because I could not tell if his Majesty might resent the manner in which I performed this service. The fundamental law of the realm forbids anybody from making water anywhere near the Palace. I was privately told that the Empress had the greatest disgust for what I had done, had moved to the farthest side of the courtyard, decided that the burned buildings should never be repaired for her use, and vowed to get revenge.

CHAPTER 6

Laws, Customs and Education in Lilliput

I INTEND TO WRITE ANOTHER WORK DESCRIBING this empire, but meanwhile I will give the reader some general ideas about it. The size of the natives is somewhat under six inches and all other animals and plants are in proportion. For instance, the tallest horses and oxen are between four and five inches high. Their geese are about the bigness of a sparrow and so on downwards until you come to the smallest things which, to me, are almost invisible. Lilliputians see with great exactness, but not very far.

Their manner of writing is very peculiar. It is not

from left to right, like the Europeans, or from right to left, like the Arabians, or from top to bottom, like the Chinese, but on a slant from one corner of the paper to the other.

Some laws and customs in this empire are very peculiar. The first I shall mention relates to informers. All crimes against the state are punished here very severely. But if the person accused makes his innocence plain at his trial, the accuser is immediately put to a shameful death. And the innocent person is paid back for his hardship and the cost of his defense out of the goods and lands of the accuser.

They look on fraud as a worse crime than theft and usually punish it with death. They say care, watchfulness and common sense can preserve a man's goods from thieves, but honesty has no protection against cunning. Since buying and selling must go on, if fraud is not punished, the honest dealer always suffers and cheaters have the advantage.

We usually call reward and punishment the two hinges on which all government turns, yet Lilliput is the only nation where I have ever seen this maxim put into practice. Whoever can prove he has strictly followed the laws for seventy-three moons can claim certain privileges and a sum of money from a fund set aside for that use. He is also given the title of Snilpall or Legal to add to his name.

In choosing persons for employment they put more value on good morals than great abilities. They suppose truth, justice, and temperance to be in every man's power. The practice of these virtues, along with experience and good intention, qualifies a man to serve, except where special training is needed. Lack of morals is not made up for by superior mental abilities, they believe. Such people should not be given important duties because of the dangerous consequences for the public welfare. Such practices as rope dancing and creeping and leaping around sticks are new institutions introduced in the reign of the grandfather of the present Emperor.

Ingratitude is a capital crime to them. They reason that if someone is unkind to someone who has been generous to him, he must be a common enemy of the rest of mankind, who have not given him anything. Therefore such a man is not fit to live.

Their notions of the duties of parents and children are very different from ours. They think the ten-

THE NURSERIES FOR BOYS OF NOBLE FAMILIES
HAVE GRAVE AND LEARNED PROFESSORS.

derness of parents toward their young comes from natural feeling. A child is not under any duty to his father
or his mother for bringing him into the world. Their
opinion is that parents are the last to be trusted with
the education of their children. Every town has public

nurseries where all parents, except laborers, must send their children to be educated once they come to the age of twenty moons.

The nurseries for boys of noble families have grave and learned professors. The clothes and food of the children are plain and simple. They are taught the principles of honor, justice, courage, modesty, mercy, religion, and love of their country. They are always busy, except in the short times for eating or sleeping and the two hours for physical exercises. Their professors are always present. Their parents are allowed to visit them twice a year for an hour at a time. Their parents can kiss them on greeting and at parting, but they may not whisper to their children, use affectionate words, or bring them presents or sweets.

The nurseries for children of gentlemen and merchants are managed in the same manner, only their children are put out as apprentices at seven years old.

The girls of noble families are educated like the boys, and if their nurses ever entertain the girls with foolish stories, they are publicly whipped three times around the city, put in prison for a year, and then banished for life to the most desolate part of the country.

ONE DAY HIS IMPERIAL MAJESTY WISHED THAT HE AND HIS FAMILY
MIGHT HAVE THE HAPPINESS (AS HE CALLED IT) OF DINING WITH ME.

Thus young ladies are as ashamed of being cowards and
fools as young men and despise personal ornaments.
When the girls are twelve years old, which is the age at

which they can marry, their parents take them home.

Laborers keep their children at home. Since their business is to farm, their education is of little importance to the public. But the old and diseased among them are cared for by hospitals. Begging is unknown in this empire.

One day his Imperial Majesty wished that he and his family might have the happiness (as he called it) of dining with me. They came and I placed them in their chairs on my table, surrounded by their guards. Flimnap, the Lord High Treasurer, came as well with his staff. He often looked at me with sour expressions, which I pretended I did not notice. I ate more than usual, to honor my dear country as well as to fill them with admiration. I believe this visit gave Flimnap an opportunity of speaking against me to his Majesty. That minister had always been my secret enemy, although he outwardly caressed me. He spoke to the Emperor of the low condition of his treasury and that I had cost his Majesty more than a million Spruggs, their gold coin, and that, on the whole, it would be prudent of the Emperor to take the first chance of getting rid of me.

CHAPTER 7

Escape to Blefescu

BEFORE I TELL OF MY LEAVING THIS KINGDOM, I must inform the reader of an intrigue against me which had been forming for two months.

Just when I was preparing to pay my call on the Emperor of Blefuscu, an important person at court (for whom I had done a favor at a time when his Majesty was displeased with him) came to my house secretly one night and wished to come in. I put his Lordship in my coat pocket and gave orders to a trusty servant to say that I had gone to sleep. Then I fastened the door of my house, put his Lordship on the table and sat down beside it. I saw his Lordship's face was full of worry and asked the reason for it. He asked me to listen to him pa-

YOU ARE AWARE THAT SKYRESH BOLGOLAM, THE HIGH ADMIRAL,
HAS BEEN YOUR DEADLY ENEMY SINCE YOUR ARRIVAL.

tiently about something that concerned my honor and
my life. I made notes of his speech as soon as he left.

"Several committees of Council have been called
in secret on your account," he said, "and two days ago
his Majesty came to a decision.

"You are aware that Skyresh Bolgolam, the High Admiral, has been your deadly enemy since your arrival. His hatred has grown since your success against Blefuscu, which overshadowed his own glory. This lord, with Flimnap, the High Treasurer and others, has accused you of treason and other crimes."

Hearing this made me want to interrupt him, since I was sure of my innocence, but he motioned to me to be silent and then went on.

"Out of gratitude for favors you have done me, I have risked my life to bring you a copy of the charges."

THE CHARGES AGAINST QUINBUS FLESTRIN, THE MAN MOUNTAIN

I. Quinbus Flestrin in openly breaking the law against making water in the courtyards of the Royal Palace, under the appearance of putting out a fire in the apartment of her Majesty, did traitorously and devilishly, by discharge of urine, put out said fire in said apartment within the courtyards of said Palace.

II. Said Quinbus Flestrin, having brought the fleet of Blefuscu to the Royal Port and being commanded by his Majesty to seize all the other ships of the Empire of Blefuscu, to

*make that empire into a subject province, and to put to death
all Big-End exiles and all who would not forsake the Big-End
belief; he, the said Flestrin, like a false traitor, did excuse himself from said service by pretending to be unwilling to destroy
the liberties and lives of innocent people.*

*III. Whereas certain ambassadors from the court of
Blefuscu came to his Majesty to ask for peace, the said Flestrin,
like a false traitor, did entertain said ambassadors even though
he knew they were servants of an enemy lately at war against
his said Majesty.*

*IV. The said Quinbus Flestrin, contrary to the duty of a
faithful subject, is preparing to visit the Empire of Blefuscu,
with only spoken permission from his Majesty, and with the
appearance of such permission, does traitorously intend to
make said visit and thereby aid the Emperor of Blefuscu, lately an enemy at war against his said Majesty.*

"There are other charges, but these are the most
important.

"In the debates over these charges his Majesty
gave many signs of his mercy. He often brought up services you had done for him and tried to excuse the seri-
ousness of your crimes. The Treasurer and the Admiral

insisted you should be put to a painful death by setting
your house on fire at night. The General was to be present with twenty thousand men armed with poison
arrows to shoot you on the face and hands. Some of your
servants would be secretly ordered to pour poison juice
on your shirts that would make you want to tear off your
own flesh and die in extreme torture. The General was of
the same opinion. But his Majesty preferred, if possible,
to spare your life.

"At this point, Reldresal, the secretary for private
affairs, your true friend, was commanded by the Emperor
to give his opinion.

"He agreed your crimes are serious, but that still
there is room for mercy, the virtue for which his Majesty
is so justly celebrated. He said the friendship between you
and him is so well-known that perhaps the board might
think him partial. However, he would freely offer his feel-
ings. He suggested that if his Majesty, considering your
services to him and since he is so merciful, would spare
your life and only give an order to put out your eyes, justice might be satisfied. All the world would applaud this
show of mercy as well as the fairness and generosity of
the councilors. The loss of your eyes would not reduce

your bodily strength, so you might still be useful to his Majesty. Blindness would add to your courage by concealing danger from you. The fear you had of injury to your eyes was the greatest difficulty in bringing over the enemy's fleet and it would be enough for you to see through the eyes of the ministers, just as the great kings do.

"This idea was strongly disapproved of by the council. Bolgolam could not keep his temper. Rising up in fury, he wondered how the secretary could suggest saving the life of a traitor. The way you had put out the fire in the Queen's apartment, he said with horror, showed you could do the same thing to drown the whole Palace. You might, if you became unhappy, take the enemy's fleet back. And he strongly suspected you are a Big-Endian in your heart, the place where treason begins. He insisted that you should be put to death.

"The treasurer agreed. He said the cost of feeding you would soon be unaffordable. Blinding you would probably increase costs, as shown by the common practice of blinding chickens, after which they eat more and grow fat sooner.

"But his Majesty decided against capital punishment. Since the council thought the loss of your eyes was too easy a penalty, he said graciously, something more may be done afterward. Your friend the secretary then said that, as far as the drain on the treasury was concerned, his Majesty might gradually lessen the amount of food given to you, which would make you grow faint and weak, lose your appetite and waste away in a few months. The stench of your carcass would not be so dangerous because your body would be shrunk to half its present size. Five or six thousand subjects could cut your flesh from your bones in two or three days and bury it to prevent infection. Your skeleton would be left as a monument.

"Thus a compromise was reached. The project of starving you is to be kept secret, but the sentence of putting out your eyes will be entered on the books.

"In three days, your friend the secretary will come to your house, read the charges to you, and tell you of his Majesty's great mercy: that you lose only your eyes. His Majesty expects you to submit gratefully to this. Twenty of his Majesty's surgeons will come along to see that very sharp arrows are shot into your eyes as you lie on the ground.

"I leave it to you to decide what to do. To avoid suspicion I must immediately leave as secretly as I came."

I remained alone with many doubts.

It was a custom of this Emperor, after ordering a cruel execution, to make a speech expressing his mercy and tenderness. This speech was immediately published throughout the kingdom. Nothing terrified the people so much as these praises of the Emperor's mercy, because the more the Emperor's mercy was insisted on, the more barbaric was the punishment and the more likely that the one who suffered it was innocent.

I must confess, not being used to courts, that I could not find the mercy in this sentence. I thought about resisting. While I was free, the whole strength of the empire could hardly control me and I might easily pelt the city to pieces with stones. But I soon rejected that plan with horror, remembering my promise not to hurt the people.

At last I decided what to do. I sent a letter to my friend the secretary telling him I was setting out that morning for Blefuscu, as I had been given permission to do. Without waiting for an answer, I went to the coast where the fleet lay. I seized a warship and tied a cable to it. I stripped myself and put my clothes and coverlet in the vessel. By wading and swimming I came to the port of Blefuscu.

The people had long expected me. They gave me two guides to take me to the capital. I held them in my hands until we came within two hundred yards of the city gate, and then I sent them ahead to announce my arrival. In about an hour his Majesty, with his royal family and others from the court, came out to receive me. I lay on the ground to kiss his Majesty's and the Empress's hands. I told him I came according to my promise, with the permission of my master, and offered any service in my power. I did not mention a word of my disgrace because I was not yet supposed to know about it.

CHAPTER 8

Gulliver Returns to His Native Country

T HREE DAYS AFTER MY ARRIVAL, EXPLORING the northeast coast of the island, I saw, about a mile off in the sea, something that looked like an overturned boat. I took off my shoes and socks and waded out about three hundred yards. The object was being brought nearer by the tide. Then I plainly saw it was a boat, which I supposed had been lost from a ship in a storm.

I returned immediately to the city and asked his Majesty to lend me twenty of the tallest ships he had left and three thousand sailors. While this fleet sailed around, I went back the shortest way to the coast where I first found the boat. The tide had driven it still nearer.

The sailors all had ropes which I had twisted together beforehand. When the ships came up, I stripped and waded out until I was forced to swim to get to the boat. The sailors threw me an end of the rope, which I fastened to a hole in the front of the boat, and the other end to a warship. Since I was unable to touch the bottom, I could do no work. I swam behind and pushed the boat forward as often as I could. When I got to a depth that I could touch the bottom and hold my chin out of the water, I rested a few minutes and then gave the boat another shove. The hardest work was over. Now I took other cables and tied them, first to the boat and then to nine other vessels. The wind was favorable. The sailors towed and I pushed until we arrived at the shore. When the tide was out, with the assistance of two thousand men with ropes, I turned the boat on its bottom and found it was only slightly damaged.

It took me ten days to make paddles and with them I got the boat to the royal port, where a large crowd appeared, full of wonder at the sight of so huge a vessel. I told the Emperor that good fortune had thrown this

WITH THE ASSISTANCE OF TWO THOUSAND MEN WITH ROPES,
I TURNED THE BOAT ON ITS BOTTOM.

boat my way to carry me back to my own country. I
begged him for materials to fix it up and permission to
leave, which, after some discussion, he granted.

I did wonder, all this time, that no message relat-
ed to me arrived from our Emperor to the court of
Blefuscu. Later I was told that the Emperor, never imag-
ining that I knew of his plans, believed I had gone to

Blefuscu according to the permission he had given me and would return in a few days. But at last he became upset by my long absence and, after consulting the Treasurer, he sent a copy of the charges against me to Blefuscu. His envoy was to explain to the monarch of Blefuscu that my merciful master only wanted to punish me by putting out my eyes. I had fled from justice and if I did not return in two hours, I would be declared a traitor. The envoy added that in order to keep peace between the empires his master expected that his Brother of Blefuscu would send me back to Lilliput bound hand and foot.

The Emperor of Blefuscu took three days to consult and sent back an answer consisting of polite excuses. As for sending me bound, that was impossible. And, although I had taken away his fleet, he owed me for my help in making the peace. Besides, I had found a huge vessel on the shore, big enough to carry me to sea, and he hoped in a few weeks both empires would be freed of the burden of me.

With this answer the envoy returned to Lilliput. The monarch of Blefuscu told me all that had happened. He offered me his gracious protection if I would serve him. I believe he was sincere, yet I resolved never to trust kings and ministers if I could possibly avoid it. I humbly begged to be excused. I told him that since fortune, for good or bad, had thrown a vessel my way, I would venture on the ocean rather than be the cause of differences between two mighty monarchs. The Emperor was not unhappy; in fact, he was very glad.

These reasons caused me to hasten my departure. The court, impatient to have me gone, helped readily. Five hundred workmen were employed to make two sails for my boat and I made ropes by twisting together the strongest of theirs. A great stone I happened to find served as an anchor. I had the fat of three hundred cows for greasing my boat. I had a great deal of trouble cutting down timber trees for oars and masts, but I was helped by his Majesty's carpenters, who smoothed them after I had done the rough work.

In about a month, when all was prepared, I went to his Majesty to take my leave. The Emperor and Royal Family came out of the palace. I lay down on my face to kiss his hand, which he offered to me. So did the Empress. His Majesty gave me fifty purses containing two hundred Sprugs apiece and a full-length picture of him, which I put into one of my gloves to keep it from being hurt.

I stored the carcasses of a hundred oxen and three hundred sheep in the boat, as well as bread and drink. I took six living cows and two bulls, and as many ewes and rams, intending to carry them to my own country and breed them. To feed them on board I took a bundle of hay and a bag of corn. I would gladly have taken a dozen natives, but the Emperor would not allow it.

I set sail on the 24th of September, 1701, at six in the morning. When I had gone about four leagues north-ward, at six in the evening, I caught sight of a small island. I cast anchor on the sheltered side of the island, which seemed uninhabited. I took some refreshment and rested. I slept well. I ate breakfast before the sun was up, heaved the anchor, and steered the same course as the day before, guided by my pocket compass.

My intention was to reach, if possible, one of the islands I believed lay north of Van Damien's Land. I discovered nothing that day, but the next I spotted a sail steering to the southeast. I found I gained on her. In half an hour she spied me and fired a gun.

It is not easy to express the joy I felt over the hope of seeing my beloved country again. She slackened her sails and I came up with her in the evening. My heart leapt within me to see her English flag. I put my cows and sheep in my coat pockets and got on board with my little cargo of provisions.

The vessel was returning from Japan. The captain, Mr. John Biddel of Deptford, was an excellent sailor. Among the fifty men on the ship, I met an old comrade, Peter Williams, who vouched for my good character. The captain treated me kindly and asked what place I came from last. I told him in a few words, but he thought I was raving and that the dangers I lived through had disturbed my head. So I took my cattle and sheep out of my pocket, which both astonished him and clearly convinced him of my truthfulness. Then I showed him the gold given to me by the Emperor of Belfuscu as well as his Majesty's picture. I gave him two purses of Sprugs and promised to give a cow and a sheep when we reached England.

We arrived in England on the 13th of April, 1702. I had only one misfortune, that the rats on board carried away one of my sheep. I found her bones in a hole, picked clean. The rest of my cattle I got to shore safely and set them grazing on a fine lawn. In the short time I stayed in England I made a considerable profit showing my cattle, and before I began my second voyage, I sold them for six hundred pounds.

I stayed two months with my wife and family, but my intense desire to see foreign countries would allow me to stay no longer. I left fifteen hundred pounds with my wife and fixed her in a good house. I carried the rest of my money and goods with me in hopes of improving my fortune. I took leave of my wife, and boy and girl, and went aboard the *Adventure*, a merchant ship bound for **Surat**, commanded by Captain John Nicholas of Liverpool.

SURAT
A city on India's west coast where the British first established a trading post.

PART II

A Voyage to Brobdingnag

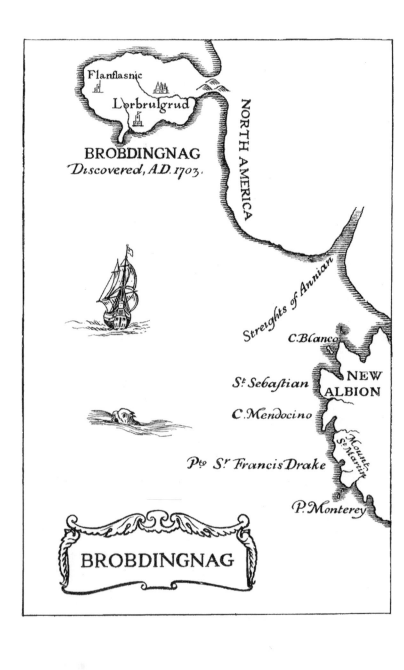

Flanflasnic

Lorbrulgrud

BROBDINGNAG
Discovered, A.D. 1703.

NORTH AMERICA

Streights of Annian

C. Blanco

St. Sebastian

NEW ALBION

C. Mendocino

Mount St. Martin

Pto Sr Francis Drake

P. Monterey

BROBDINGNAG

CHAPTER 1

Gulliver Is Left Behind on Shore and Captured by a Farmer

ONDEMNED BY NATURE TO A RESTLESS LIFE, I left my native country in the *Adventure* on the 20th of June, 1702. We had a prosperous voyage until we arrived at the **Cape of Good Hope**, where we landed to get fresh water. Discovering a leak in the ship, we unloaded our cargo and wintered there. At the end of March we set sail and had a good voyage until we passed the **Straits of Madagascar**. Then, for twenty days, strong west winds blew us a little to the east

of the **Molucca Islands**. There we encountered a fierce
storm that carried us five hundred leagues to the east, so
that the oldest sailor among us
could not tell in what part
of the world we were.
Our food held out
well, and the crew
was in good health,
but we were in des-
perate need of water.
On the 16th
day of June, 1703, a boy
on the topmast discov-
ered land. The next day we
saw a great island or a continent (we did not know
which) with a small neck of land jutting out into the
sea. We cast anchor within a league of a shallow creek
and the captain sent a dozen men, well armed, in the
long boat to find water. I asked his permission to go
with them to explore the country. When we landed, we
saw no spring nor any sign of inhabitants. Our men
wandered on the shore to find fresh water and I walked
alone about a mile in the other direction. The country

was barren and rocky. Being weary and seeing nothing to attract my curiosity, I turned back towards the creek. I saw our men already in the boat, rowing for their lives toward the ship. I was going to holler after them, when I saw a huge creature walking after them in the sea as fast as he could. He waded in not much deeper than his knees and took enormous strides. But our men had a good start and the sea there being full of sharp rocks, the monster could not catch the boat.

I dared not stay to see what happened. I ran as fast as I could in the direction I had first been going and then climbed a steep hill to get a view of the country. I found it fully cultivated, but what surprised me was that the grass kept for hay was above twenty feet high.

I fell into a high road, or so I took it to be. To the inhabitants, it was only a footpath through a field of grain. I walked on for some time, but could see little on either side because it was near harvest and the grain rose at least forty feet. It took an hour to walk to the end of this field, which was fenced in with a hedge at least one hundred and twenty feet high and trees so lofty I could not figure their height. There was a stile to pass from this field to the next. It had four steps and a stone to cross

over at the top. It was impossible for me to climb, because each step was six feet high and the upper stone
was above twenty.

I was trying to find some gap in the hedge, when
I saw one of the inhabitants in the next field coming
toward the stile. He was about the same size as the one
I saw in the sea pursuing our boat. He appeared as tall
as a church steeple and covered about ten yards in every
stride, as near as I could guess.

I was struck with extreme fear and ran to hide in
the grain. I saw him at the top of the stile, looking back
into the next field, and heard him call in a voice louder
than a trumpet. At first I thought it was thunder. Then
seven monsters like him came toward him with sickles
in their hands, each about the largeness of six scythes.
These people seemed to be laborers. They began to reap
grain in the field where I was.

I kept as far away from them as I could, but I
moved with great difficulty because the stalks were so
close together I could hardly squeeze between them.
However, I managed to go forward until I came to a part
of the field where the grain had been knocked down by
rain and wind. Here it was impossible for me to take a

step. The stalks were so interwoven I could not crawl through, and the tips of the fallen ears were so strong and pointed that they pierced through my clothes into my flesh. I could hear the reapers not a hundred yards behind me.

Dejected from toil and overcome by despair, I lay down between two ridges and wished I might end my days there. I bemoaned my lonely widow and my father-less children. I regretted my folly in taking another voy-age against the advice of all my friends and relations. I could not help thinking of Lilliput, whose people looked upon me as the greatest wonder that ever appeared in the world, where I pulled an imperial fleet in my hands and did other things that will be recorded forever in the chronicles of that empire. I thought how humiliating it was to be so insignificant in this nation, just as a single Lilliputian would be among us. But this was the least of my troubles. Just as humans are as sav-age and cruel as they are big, what could I expect but to be a morsel in the mouth of the first of these enormous barbarians who happened to grab me?

One of the reapers came within ten yards of where I lay, making me fear that with his next step I

would be squashed to death under his foot, or cut in two
with his sickle. Therefore, when he was about to move
again, I screamed as loud as fear could make me. The huge
creature took a small step, and looking around for some
time, at last spied me as I lay on the ground. He used caution, as one would in trying to lay hold of a small dangerous animal in a way that it could not scratch or bite. He
took me up with his middle finger and thumb and brought
me within three yards of his eyes to see me better. I did not
struggle in the least as he held me in the air more than
sixty feet from the ground, although he painfully pinched
my sides, for fear I would slip through his fingers. All I did
was raise my eyes, place my hands together as if I was pray-
ing, and speak in a humble tone.

I feared every moment that he would dash me
against the ground. But as my good star would have it, he
appeared pleased with my voice and gestures. He looked
on me as a curiosity, wondering at hearing me pronounce
words, even though he could not understand them. Meantime, I was not able to keep myself from groaning and cry-
ing and turning my head from side to side. I was trying to
let him know how cruelly I was hurt by his thumb and finger. He seemed to understand. Lifting up the flap of his

I PULLED OFF MY HAT AND MADE A LOW BOW TO THE FARMER.

coat pocket, he put me gently inside and ran with me to his master, who was the person I had first seen in the field.

The farmer, after hearing about me from his servant, took a small straw, about the size of a walking stick, and lifted up the lapels of my coat, which he seemed to think was some kind of covering nature gave me. He blew my hair aside to get a better view of my face. He called his laborers together and asked (so I was told later) if they had ever seen a little creature like me in the fields. He then placed me down softly on all fours. But I immediately got up and walked slowly back and forth to show that I did not intend to run away.

They all sat down in a circle around me to watch me. I pulled off my hat and made a low bow to the farmer. I fell on my knees, lifted up my hands, and spoke several words as loud as I could. I took a purse of gold out of my pocket and presented it to him. He took it in the palm of his hand and looked at it very closely, but he could make nothing of it. Then I made a sign to him to place his hand on the ground. I took the purse and poured all the gold into his palm. There were six

SPANISH PISTOLES
Gold coins.

Spanish pistoles and twenty or thirty smaller coins. I saw him wet the tip of his little finger on his tongue and take up one of my largest coins, but he did not understand what it was. He gestured to me to put them back in my purse and put the purse back in my pocket.

By this time, the farmer was convinced I must be a thinking creature. He spoke to me often, but his voice had the sound of a waterwheel to me. I answered as loud as I could in several languages, and he laid his ear within two yards of me, but all was in vain. We could not make sense of each other. He sent his servants back to work, took his handkerchief out of his pocket, spread it flat on the ground and made a sign to me to step into it, which I could easily do, since it was only one foot thick. I thought it wise to obey and I laid myself full-length on it.

In this manner he carried me home to his house. He called his wife and showed me to her, but she screamed and ran back as women do at the sight of a spider. However, when she had seen my behavior and how well I followed the signs her husband made, she was soon at ease. Gradually, she grew very tender to me.

It was noon and a servant brought in dinner. It was one large cut of meat in a dish about twenty-four feet wide. At the table were the farmer and his wife, three children and an old grandmother. When they sat down, the farmer placed me far from him on the table, which was thirty feet high from the floor. I was in a terrible fright and kept as far as I could from the edge.

The wife cut up a bit of meat, crumbled some bread on a plate, and placed it before me. I bowed to her and took out my knife and fork and began to eat, which delighted them. The wife filled a small cup, which held about two gallons. I lifted the vessel with difficulty in both hands and drank to her good health. They laughed so hard I was almost deafened by the noise. The liquid tasted like cider.

Then the master made a sign for me to come next to his dish. As I walked on the table, I happened to stumble against a crust and fell flat on my face, but was not hurt. I got up immediately and, seeing their concern, I took my hat and waved it three times over my head, yelling "hurrah" each time, to show I was not injured.

As I advanced toward my master (as I shall call him), his youngest son, a boy about ten years old, picked me up by the legs and held me so high in the air that I trembled in every limb. But his father snatched me from him and at the same time boxed his left ear, ordering him away from the table. Afraid the boy might now dislike me, remembering how mischievous all our children are to sparrows, rabbits, kittens and puppies,

IN THE MIDDLE OF DINNER, MY MISTRESS'S
FAVORITE CAT LEAPT INTO HER LAP.

I fell on my knees and pointed at the boy. I made my
master understand I wished his son might be pardoned. His father did so and the lad took his seat
again. I went to him and kissed his hand, and in return
his father made him stroke me gently.

In the middle of dinner, my mistress's favorite cat leapt into her lap. I heard a noise behind me like that of a dozen weavers at work and, turning my head, I found it was the purring of this animal. She was three times the size of an ox. Her mistress was feeding and stroking her. The fierceness of this creature's face completely unnerved me, even though I was at the other end of the table, fifty feet away, and my mistress held her fast for fear she might spring and seize me in her talons. But there was no danger, because the cat took no notice of me. As I have always been told, and found true by experience in my travels, running away or showing fear to a fierce animal is a certain way to make it chase or attack you. So I resolved on this dangerous occasion to show no sort of concern. I walked bravely in front of the cat five or six times. I came within a yard of her and she drew back, as if she were afraid of me. I was less afraid of the dogs, three or four of which came into the room, as is usual in farmers' houses. One dog was as big as four elephants.

When dinner was almost done, a nurse came in with an infant child in her arms, who saw me and began a squall that you might have heard **from London Bridge to**

FROM LONDON BRIDGE TO CHELSEA
A distance of about 3.5 miles.

THE CHILD GRABBED ME BY THE MIDDLE
AND GOT MY HEAD IN HIS MOUTH.

Chelsea in order to get me as a toy. The mother, spoiling the baby, took me and put me toward the child, who grabbed me by the middle and got my head in his mouth.

I roared so loud the brat was frightened and let me drop.
I certainly would have broken my neck if the mother had
not caught me in her apron.

When dinner was done my master went out to
his laborers and, as I could make out from his gestures,
gave his wife orders to take care of me. I was very tired
and wanted to sleep, which my mistress perceived. She
put me on her own bed and covered me with a clean
white handkerchief, larger and coarser than the main sail
on a warship.

I slept about two hours and dreamed I was at
home with my wife and children, which increased my
sorrow when I awoke and found myself alone in the vast
room, three hundred feet wide and two hundred feet
high, lying in a bed twenty yards wide. I had been locked
in. The bed was eight yards from the floor. And some
natural necessities required me to get down.

While I was in these circumstances, two rats
crept up the curtains and ran back and forth on the bed.
One of them came up almost to my face. I rose in fright
and drew my sword to defend myself. These horrible animals attacked me from both sides. One of them put his
front feet on my collar, but I ripped up his belly before he

I GAVE HIM A GOOD WOUND IN HIS BACK
THAT MADE BLOOD RUN FROM HIM AS HE FLED.

could harm me. He fell down at my feet. The other one, seeing the fate of his friend, made his escape, but not before I gave him a good wound in his back that made blood run from him as he fled. After this feat, I walked to and fro on the bed to catch my breath. These creatures were the size of large dogs, but far more nimble and fierce. If I had taken off my sword before I went to sleep, I surely would have been torn to pieces and eaten. I measured the tail of the dead rat and found it two yards long. It went against my stomach to drag the carcass off the bed. It was still bleeding. I saw signs of life still in it, so I slashed it across the neck and finally killed it.

Soon my mistress came in the room. Seeing me all bloody, she ran and took me in her hand. I pointed to the dead rat, smiling to show I was not hurt. She rejoiced and told the maid to pick up the dead rat with a pair of tongs and throw it out the window. Then she set me on the table. I showed her my bloody sword and, wiping it on my coattail, I returned it to my scabbard.

I still needed to do one thing. Bashfully, I pointed to the door and bowed several times. At last the good woman understood me and, taking me up, walked into the garden and set me down. I motioned to her not to look and, hiding behind two leaves, I did the necessities of nature.

CHAPTER 2

Gulliver Goes
to Town

MY MISTRESS HAD A DAUGHTER NINE
years old, a child who showed promise, expert with her needle and skillful
at dressing her doll. Her mother and
she managed to fit up the doll's cradle for me to sleep
in. The cradle was put in a small drawer of a cabinet,
and the drawer was placed on a hanging shelf that was
safe from the rats. This was my bed while I stayed with
those people. It gradually became more comfortable as
I learned their language and was able to make my
wants known.

This young girl made me seven shirts and some other clothing of as fine a material as could be got, which indeed was coarser than **sackcloth**. These she washed for me with her hands. She also taught me the language. When I pointed to anything, she told me the name of it in her own tongue, so that in a few days I was able to call for whatever I had a mind to. She was good-natured and not above forty feet high, being little for her age.

SACK-CLOTH
A coarse cloth, such as burlap.

She gave me the name Grildrig, which the family took up, and afterwards the whole kingdom did too. The word means the same as the English word manikin. To her I owe my survival in that country. We never parted while I was there. I called her Glumdalclitch, meaning little nurse. I would be ungrateful if I failed to mention her care and affection for me. I heartily wish it were in my power to repay her as she deserves, instead of being the cause of her disgrace, as I fear I am.

It now began to be talked about in the neighborhood that my master had found a strange animal in the field, shaped exactly like a human creature and also acting like one. It seemed to speak a little language, had already learned several words of theirs, walked on two

I COULD NOT HELP LAUGHING VERY HEARTILY. HIS EYES APPEARED LIKE
THE FULL MOON SHINING INTO A ROOM THROUGH TWO WINDOWS.

legs, was tame and gentle, would come when it was
called and do whatever it was asked.

Another farmer, who lived close by and was a
good friend of my master, visited on purpose to find out
the truth of this story. I was brought out and placed on

the table. I walked as I was commanded, drew my sword and put it away again. I was respectful of my master's guest, asked him in his own language how he did and told him he was welcome, just as my little nurse had instructed me. This man, who was old and had poor eyesight, put on his spectacles to see me better. I could not help laughing very heartily. His eyes appeared like the full moon shining into a room through two windows. Our people, who discovered why I was laughing, joined in it, and the old fellow became angry.

He had the character of a miser and, to my misfortune, he deserved it. He advised my master to exhibit me on a market day in the next town. I guessed there was some mischief brewing when I saw my master and his friend whispering together and sometimes pointing at me. The next morning Glumdalclitch told me the whole matter, which she had found out from her mother.

The poor girl laid me on her bosom and began weeping from grief. She was afraid some mischief would happen to me from rude folks, who might squeeze me to death or break one of my limbs by taking me in their hands. She had seen how modest I was, how careful I was of my honor, and imagined how disgraced I would feel to be exposed for money as a public spectacle. She said her Papa and Mamma had promised Grildrig would be hers. But now she found they meant to treat her as they did last year when they pretended to give her a lamb, and yet as soon as it was fat, they sold it to a butcher.

For my part, I can truthfully say I was less concerned than my nurse. I had a strong hope, which never left me, that I would one day have my liberty again. As to the humiliation of being carried around for show, I considered myself a stranger in the country and such bad luck could never be considered a disgrace if ever I returned to England, since the king himself, in my situation, must have undergone the same thing.

My master carried me in a box the next market day to the nearby town and took along his daughter, my nurse. The box was closed on every side, with a little door for me to go in and out, and a few small holes to let in air. The girl had put the quilt from her doll bed in it for me to lie down on. However, I was terribly shaken on this journey, even though it took only half an hour. The horse went about forty feet in each step and trotted so high that the shaking was like the rising and falling of a ship in a storm.

My master stopped at an inn and, after talking with the innkeeper and making some preparations, he hired a **crier** to give notice through the town that a strange creature, who looked like a human and could speak words and perform tricks, could be seen at the sign of the Green Eagle.

CRIER
A person who went through town shouting announcements.

I was placed on a table in the largest room of the inn, which was about three hundred feet square. My little nurse stood on a low stool next to the table to take care of me and tell me what to do. My master would let in only thirty people at a time to see me. I walked around on the table as she commanded. She asked me questions she knew I could understand and I answered as loud as I could. I made some other speeches I had been taught, and I took up a thimble filled with liquor that Glumdalclitch had given to me and drank to their health. I drew out my sword and waved it boldly. That day I was shown to twelve sets of people and forced to go over the same foolishness each time until I was half dead. Those who had already seen me made such wonderful reports that people were ready to break down the doors to get in. My master would not allow anyone to touch me except my nurse. To prevent danger, benches were set around the table at a distance that put me out of everybody's reach. However, a school boy aimed a hazelnut at my head that just missed. Otherwise, it would have knocked out my brains, since it was as large as a pumpkin. I had the satisfaction to see the young rogue beaten and thrown out of the room.

My master gave public notice that he would show me again the next market day. In the meantime, he made a more comfortable vehicle for me, which he had good reason to do. I was so tired from my journey and from entertaining company, I could hardly stand on my legs or speak a word. It was at least three days before I recovered my strength. But I had almost no rest at home. Neighboring families from one hundred miles around came to see me at my master's own house.

My master, finding how profitable I was likely to be, decided to carry me to the largest cities in the kingdom. He took leave of his wife on the 17th of August, 1703, two months after I arrived, and we set out for the capital, which is in the middle of that empire, and about three thousand miles from our house. Glumdalclitch carried me on her lap in a box tied to her waist. She had lined it on all sides with the softest cloth she could get and made everything as comfortable as she could. A boy rode behind us with the luggage.

My master's plan was to show me in all the towns on the way and to go off the main road for fifty or one hundred miles to any village or manor where he might find customers. Glumdalclitch, in order to spare me, frequently complained that she was tired of the trotting of the horse. She often took me out of the box to give me air and show me the country, but she always held me with strings. We passed over five or six rivers much broader and deeper than the Nile or the Ganges. Hardly a creek was so small as the Thames at London Bridge. We were ten weeks on our journey and I was shown in eighteen large towns, besides many villages and private houses.

On the 26th of October, 1703, we arrived in the capital, called Lorbrulgrud, which means "pride of the universe." My master took a lodging in the principal street of the city, near the royal Palace, and put out posters describing me and my abilities. He rented a large room four hundred feet wide. He put a table in it for me to perform on and fenced it around, three feet from the edge, to prevent me from falling. I was shown ten times a day to the wonder of all people. I could now speak the

SHE OFTEN TOOK ME OUT OF THE BOX TO GIVE ME AIR AND SHOW ME THE COUNTRY, BUT SHE ALWAYS HELD ME WITH STRINGS.

language fairly well and could understand any word spoken to me. Glumdalclitch had been my teacher while we were at home and during our journey.

CHAPTER 3

Gulliver at the Royal Court

THE MANY LABORS I DID EVERY DAY MADE A very considerable change in my health in a few weeks. The more my master earned by me, the more greedy he grew. I had quite lost my appetite and was almost reduced to a skeleton. The farmer saw it and, figuring I soon must die, decided to make as much money from me as he could. While he was reasoning with himself in this way, a gentleman came from court commanding my master to bring me there immediately to entertain the Queen and her ladies. Some of the ladies had already seen me and reported

THIS GRACIOUS PRINCESS HELD OUT HER LITTLE FINGER TO ME,
WHICH I EMBRACED WITH BOTH ARMS. I PUT THE TIP OF IT,
WITH THE GREATEST RESPECT, TO MY LIPS.

strange things of my beauty, behavior and good sense.

Her Majesty and those with her were very delighted with me. I fell on my knees and begged for the honor of kissing the royal foot. But this gracious princess held out her little finger to me, which I embraced with both arms. I put the tip of it, with the greatest respect, to my lips. She asked me some general questions about my country and my travels, which I answered as clearly and in as few words as possible. She asked whether I would be content to live at court. I bowed down to the table and said humbly that I was my master's slave, but if I could choose for myself, I would be proud to devote my life to her Majesty's service.

She then asked my master if he was willing to sell me. He, who feared I could not live a month, was ready to part with me and demanded a thousand pieces of gold. They were ordered to him on the spot.

I then said to the Queen, since I was now her humble servant, that I must beg the favor that Glumdalclitch, who always tended to me with so much care and kindness and knew how to do it so well, might continue as my nurse and instructor. Her Majesty agreed to my request and easily got the farmer's consent, who was glad to have his daughter at the royal court. The poor girl herself was not able to hide her joy. My old master left, saying farewell to me, and that he left me in a good position. I replied not a word, only making him a slight bow.

The Queen noticed my coldness, and when the farmer was gone out of the room, she asked me the reason for it. I told her boldly that I owed nothing to my former master, other than that he did not dash out the brains of a poor harmless creature he found by chance in his field. He had been repaid by the money he made showing me through half the kingdom and the price he sold me for. The life I led was enough hard labor to kill an animal ten times my strength. My health was injured by the drudgery of entertaining crowds every hour of the day, and that if my master had not thought my life was in danger, her Majesty perhaps would not have gotten so cheap a bargain. I said I did not fear being ill-treated while protected by so great and good an empress, who was the ornament of nature, the darling of the world, the delight of her people, and the **Phoenix** of creation. I already found my spirits lifted by her presence.

PHOENIX
The name of a legendary bird that was burned to ashes and then rose alive.

This was my speech, delivered with great hesitation. The last part was in the style of those people, using phrases I had learned from Glumdalclitch.

The Queen, allowing for my poor speaking, was surprised that so much good sense was in so tiny an animal. She took me in her hand and carried me to the King, who was in his private room. His Majesty, a prince of stern looks, not seeing my shape well at first glance, asked the Queen, coldly, how long she had been fond of Splacknucks. But this princess set me gently on the desk and commanded me to tell his Majesty about myself, which I did. Glumdalclitch, who was waiting outside the door and could not stand for me to be out of her sight, was allowed in and confirmed all that had happened since I came to her father's house.

The King, although he had been educated in philosophy and mathematics, when he looked at my shape closely and saw me walk, thought I might be a piece of clockwork made by some clever artist. But when he heard my voice, he could not hide his astonishment. He was not at all satisfied with the story I told him of how I came into his kingdom. He thought it was a story agreed upon by Glumdalclitch and her father, who taught me to

HIS MAJESTY SENT FOR THREE PROFESSORS, WHO AFTER THEY
EXAMINED ME CLOSELY, HAD DIFFERENT OPINIONS ABOUT ME.

say a set of words in order to make me sell at a higher price. With this in mind, he asked me several other questions and I gave reasonable answers.

His Majesty sent for three professors who, after they examined me closely, had different opinions about me. They all agreed I could not be made according to the usual laws of nature because I was not made with the ability to save my life by swiftness, climbing trees or digging holes in the earth. They saw from my teeth, which they studied very closely, that I was a meat-eating animal. Yet most four-legged animals would be too powerful for me and mice too nimble, so they could not imagine how I might feed myself, unless I ate snails and insects. They did not think I was a dwarf because my littleness was beyond all comparison. The Queen's favorite dwarf, the smallest ever known in that kingdom, was nearly thirty feet high. After much debate, they decided I was a Relplum Scalcath, which means freak of nature.

After they made this decision, I asked to be heard. I assured his Majesty that I came from a country that had several million people of my stature, where the trees, animals and houses were all in proportion. There I was able to defend myself and find food as well as any of his Majesty's subjects could do here. To this the scholars only sneered, saying that the farmer had instructed me well in my story.

The King, who had a much better mind, dismissed his scholars and sent for the farmer, who fortunately had not yet gone out of town. Having questioned him privately, his Majesty began to think that what we told him might possibly be true. He desired the Queen to take special care of me and thought Glumdalclitch should continue to tend to me, because he saw we had a great affection for each other. An apartment was provided for her at court. She had a governess to oversee her education, a maid to dress her and two other servants. But the care of me was entirely her duty.

The Queen commanded her cabinetmaker to make a box, according to my plans, that would be my bedroom. This man was an artist, who in three weeks finished a wooden chamber sixteen feet square, with **sash windows**, a door and two closets. The board that was the ceiling opened and closed on two hinges, to put in a bed. Glumdalclitch took it out every day to air out and put it back at night when she locked the roof over me. A

SASH WINDOWS
Windows with panes in a frame, often moveable.

workman, who was famous for little knickknacks, made me two chairs from a substance like ivory, two tables and a wardrobe to put my things in. The room was quilted on all sides, as well as the floor and ceiling, to prevent accidents from the carelessness of those who carried me. I asked for a lock for my door to prevent rats and mice from coming in.

The Queen also ordered the thinnest silks available to make me clothes. They were as thick as blankets and cumbersome until I got used to them. They were in the fashion of the kingdom and looked Persian or Chinese.

The Queen became so fond of me that she could not dine without me. I had a table and chair placed on her table, at her left elbow. Glumdalclitch stood on a stool on the floor near my table. I had an entire set of silver dishes which, compared to the Queen's plates, were not much bigger than what I have seen in London toy shops that sell doll house furniture. These my little nurse kept in her pocket in a silver box. No one dined with the Queen but the two princesses, one sixteen years old at the time and the other thirteen. Her Majesty used to put a bit of meat on my dish, which I cut for myself. Her entertainment was to see me eat in miniature. The Queen took up as much in one mouthful as a dozen English farmers could eat at a meal. For a long time, that sight made me feel like throwing up. She would crunch the wings of a bird, bones and all, between her teeth, even though it was nine times as large as a turkey. She put a bit of bread in her mouth as large as two loaves. She drank more than a hogshead at a time out of a golden cup.

Every Wednesday (which was their **Sabbath**) the King and Queen and the princesses dined together in his Majesty's apartment. At these times my little chairs and table were placed at his left hand, next to one of his salt shakers. The King took pleasure in talking to me, asking about the manners, religion, laws, government and learning of Europe. His mind was so clear and his judgment so exact that he said many wise things about what I told him.

SABBATH
The day reserved by a religion as a day for worship and rest.

But once, after I had talked a little too long about my beloved country, our trade and wars, our religion and politics, he could not resist taking me up in his hand and stroking me. After a fit of laughing, he said to one of his ministers, "How sorry a thing is human grandeur, that it could be copied by such tiny insects. And yet, I dare say, those creatures have their titles and badges of honor, their little nests and burrows that they call houses and cities. They have fashions, they love, they fight, they argue, they cheat, they betray." As he went on, my face turned red with outrage to hear my noble country, the home of virtue, piety, honor and truth, the pride and envy of the world, so insulted.

Nothing angered and embarrassed me so much as the Queen's dwarf. Being the shortest that was ever in that country, he became proud and rude at seeing a creature so much beneath him. He would always try to swagger and look big as he passed by me. He rarely failed to say a stinging word or two about my littleness. I could only revenge myself by calling him brother, or challenging him to wrestle.

He once played me a nasty trick, which set the Queen laughing, although at the same time she was angry. Her Majesty had set a soup bone she had finished with on her plate. The dwarf, seeing his opportunity while Glumdalclitch had gone to the sideboard, stood on the stool she used to take care of me at meals, took me in both hands, squeezed my legs together and wedged me in the soup bone up to my waist. I looked very ridiculous.

THE QUEEN'S DWARF WEDGED ME IN THE SOUP BONE UP TO MY WAIST.

It was more than a minute before anyone knew what happened to me, because I thought it was too embarrassing to cry out. At my request, the dwarf got no other punishment than a sound whipping.

One day at dinner, this nasty little cub was so nettled with something I said to him that, climbing up the frame of her Majesty's chair, he took me up around the middle, meaning no harm, and let me drop in a large silver bowl of cream. Then he ran away as fast as he could. If I had not been a good swimmer, it might have gone hard for me. Glumdalclitch happened to be at the other end of the room and the Queen was in such a fright she could not think to help me. But my little nurse ran to save me, after I had swallowed more than a quart of cream. I was put to bed, but had no damage other than the loss of my clothes, which were spoiled. The dwarf was whipped and forced to drink up the bowl of cream in which he had thrown me. He was never back in favor. Soon after this, the Queen gave him to one of her ladies and I saw him no more.

I was often teased by the Queen about being afraid. She used to ask me if the people of my country were as cowardly as me. The cause was this. The kingdom was pestered with flies in the summer and these stinking insects, each of them as big as a pigeon, hardly let me eat dinner with their continual humming and buzzing about my ears. They would sometimes land on my food and leave their revolting droppings and eggs. These were plain to see to me, though the natives of that country could not see small objects as well. Sometimes they

MORE THAN TWENTY WASPS, DRAWN BY THE SMELL, CAME FLYING INTO
THE ROOM, HUMMING LOUDER THAN THE SOUND OF AS MANY BAGPIPES.

would attach to my nose or forehead and sting me to
agony. I could easily see that greasy matter that allows

those creatures to walk with their feet on a ceiling. I had much trouble defending myself against these hateful animals and was always startled when they came on my face. It was not unusual for the dwarf to catch several of these insects in his hand and let them out suddenly under my nose, on purpose to frighten me and amuse the Queen. I tried to cut them to pieces with my knife as they flew, and my skill at this was much admired.

I remember one morning when Glumdalclitch set me in my box on a window, as she usually did on fair days. I lifted up my sashes and sat down at the table to eat a piece of cake for breakfast. More than twenty wasps, drawn by the smell, came flying into the room, humming louder than the sound of as many bagpipes. Some of them took the cake and carried it away in pieces. Others flew around my head and face, confusing me with noise and terrifying me with the possibility of being stung. However, I had the courage to draw my sword and attack them. I killed four, but the rest got away. These insects are as large as doves. Their stingers are an inch and a half long and as sharp as needles. I carefully saved them and have shown them with other curiosities around Europe.

CHAPTER 4

A Description
of the Country

I WILL NOW GIVE THE READER A SHORT DESCRIPTION of this country, as far as I travelled in it, which was not more than two thousand miles around Lorbrulgrud, the capital.

The King's dominions reach about six thousand miles in length and between three to five thousand miles in width. The kingdom is a peninsula, ringed to the northeast by a ridge of mountains thirty miles high, which are impossible to cross because of the volcanoes on their tops. No one knows what lies beyond those mountains. The other three sides are surrounded by the ocean.

There are no seaports in the whole kingdom. The coast is so full of pointed rocks and the sea is so rough that these people are totally cut off from the rest of the world. But the large rivers are full of vessels and abound with fish. They seldom get fish from the sea because the sea fish are the same size as those in Europe and so not worth catching. The reason nature gives such extraordinary size to plants and animals only in this land, I leave to philosophers to determine. However, now and then they take a whale that happens to be dashed against the rocks and feed on it heartily. I have known these whales to be so large a man can hardly carry one. I saw one in a dish on the King's table but he did not seem fond of it. Indeed, I think the bigness disgusted him.

The country is well-inhabited. It contains fifty-one cities, nearly one hundred towns, and a great number of villages. Lorbrulgrud stands in almost equal parts on each side of a river. It contains over eighty thousand houses. Its length is about fifty-four miles. I measured it myself on the royal map, which was laid on the ground for me. I paced the circumference barefoot several times and measured it pretty exactly. The King's palace is not a regular building, but a heap of buildings about seven miles around.

ONE DAY BEGGARS CROWDED AGAINST THE SIDES OF THE CARRIAGE
AND GAVE ME THE MOST HORRIBLE SIGHTS AN EYE EVER BEHELD.

A carriage was provided for Glumdalclitch and
me, in which her governess frequently took us out to see
the town or go to shops. I was carried in my box,
although the girl, at my request, would often take me out
and hold me in her hand so that I could view the houses
and people as we passed along the streets. One day beg-

gars crowded against the sides of the carriage and gave me the most horrible sights an eye ever beheld. The most hateful of all was the lice crawling on their clothes. I could see clearly their limbs and the snouts they root with like pigs. They were the first I ever saw and the sight perfectly turned my stomach.

The Queen ordered a smaller box made for me for traveling, because the other box was somewhat too large for Glumdalclitch's lap. It was made by the same artist, whom I directed. This traveling closet was an exact square with a window in the middle of three of the squares. Each window was screened with iron wire on the outside to prevent accidents on long journeys. On the fourth side, two strong staples were fixed, through which the person who carried me put a leather belt and buckled it around his waist. In journeys, when I was tired of the carriage, a servant on horseback would buckle on my box in front of him and set a cushion under it. There I had a full view of the country from my three windows. In this closet I had a hammock hung from the ceiling and two chairs and a table, neatly screwed to the floor to prevent their being tossed about.

CHAPTER 5

More Adventures, Including an Execution

I COULD HAVE LIVED HAPPY ENOUGH IN THAT country, if my littleness had not led to several ridiculous accidents. Glumdalclitch often carried me into the gardens of the court in my small box. Sometimes she would take me out and hold me in her hand or set me down to walk. I remember one day, before the dwarf left the Queen, he followed us into the gardens. My nurse set me down near some dwarf apple trees. He and I being close together, I felt a need to make a silly comparison between him and the trees. The rogue, seeing his chance when I was walking under one of the trees, shook it directly over my head and a dozen apples, each them as large as a barrel, came tumbling down about me. One of them hit me on my back as I was stooping and knocked me down flat on my face, but I was not hurt. The dwarf was pardoned at my request, because I had provoked him.

Another day, Glumdalclitch left me on a lawn to amuse myself while she walked on with her governess. In the meantime, there suddenly fell a violent shower of hail. The force of it immediately struck me to the ground. When I was down, the hailstones gave me cruel bangs all over my body, as if I had been pelted with tennis balls. I managed to creep along on all fours and sheltered myself by lying flat on my face under a border of **lemon thyme**. But I was so bruised from head to foot that I could not go out for ten days.

LEMON THYME
An herb with an aroma like lemons.

A more dangerous accident happened to me in the same garden. My little nurse, believing she had put me in a safe place, which I often urged her to do so that I might have some time alone, went to another part of the garden with her gov-

ONE OF THEM HIT ME ON MY BACK AS I WAS STOOPING
AND KNOCKED ME DOWN FLAT ON MY FACE, BUT I WAS NOT HURT.

erness and other ladies. While she was gone, a small
white spaniel belonging to one of the gardeners hap-

pened to range near where I lay. The dog, following the scent, came up and took me in his mouth. He ran straight to his master, wagging his tail, and set me gently on the ground.

He had been so well taught that he carried me between his teeth without hurting me, or even tearing my clothes. But the poor gardener, who knew me well and liked me, was in a terrible fright. He took me up gently and asked me how I did, but I was so out of breath I could not speak a word. In a few minutes, I felt better and he carried me to my nurse, who by this time had come back to the place where she had left me. She had been greatly upset when I did not appear or answer when she called. She scolded the gardener severely on account of his dog. But the whole thing was hushed up, because the girl was afraid of the Queen's anger.

This accident caused Glumdalclitch to resolve never to let me out of her sight when we were out. I had long been afraid of such a decision. Therefore, I concealed from her some unlucky adventures I had when I was left by myself. Once a hawk made a swoop at me, and if I had not bravely drawn my sword and run under a

I BROKE MY RIGHT SHIN AGAINST A SNAIL SHELL,
WHICH I HAPPENED TO STUMBLE OVER.

trellis, he would have certainly carried me away in his
talons. Another time, walking to the top of a fresh mole
hill, I fell in a hole up to my neck. I made up some lie not

worth remembering to excuse myself for spoiling my clothes. I also broke my right shin against a snail shell, which I happened to stumble over as I was walking alone, thinking about England.

I cannot tell whether I was pleased or shocked that small birds did not appear to be at all afraid of me. They would hop within a yard of me, looking for worms or other food, as if there were no other creature near them. I remember a thrush had the confidence to snatch out of my hand, with his bill, a piece of cake Glumdalclitch had just given me for breakfast. When I tried to catch these birds, they would boldly turn against me, trying to peck my fingers, and I dared not get within their reach. Then they would hop back unconcerned to hunt for worms or snails, as they did before. One day, I took a thick club and threw it with all my strength at a finch, knocking it down. Seizing it around the neck with both hands, I ran in triumph to my nurse. However, the bird had only been stunned, and recovering himself, he gave me many good boxes with his wings on the side of my head and body. Although I held him at arm's length and was out of reach of his claws, I often thought of letting him go. Soon he was taken by one of our servants, who wrung the bird's neck, and, at the Queen's command, I had the finch for dinner the next day.

One day a young gentleman, who was the nephew of my nurse's governess, came and pressed them both to see an execution. It was of the man who had murdered one of that gentleman's close friends. Glumdalclitch went much against her desire, for she was naturally tender-hearted. Although I hate such spectacles, my curiosity tempted me to see something that I thought must be extraordinary. The criminal was put in a chair on a scaffold set up for the purpose. His head was cut off with one blow from a sword about forty feet long. Such a huge amount of blood spurted up so high in the air that the great fountain at **Versailles** could not equal it for the time it lasted. And when the head fell on the scaffold floor, it gave a bounce that startled me, even though I was at least a mile away.

VERSAILLES
The royal palace of French kings.

The Queen often used to hear me talk of my sea voyages, and she would amuse me when I was sad. She asked me if I understood how to handle a sail or oar, and whether a little exercise rowing might not be good for my health. I answered that I understood both very well. Although my proper position had been as the ship's doctor, often in a pinch I was forced to work like a common sailor. But I did not see how this mattered in their country, where the smallest rowboat was equal to one of our best warships. And a boat such as I could manage would never survive on one of their rivers. The Queen said that if I would design a boat, her carpenter would make it, and she would provide a place for me to sail it.

The fellow was an ingenious workman, and in ten days he finished a pleasure boat easily able to hold eight Europeans. The Queen was so delighted by it that she ran with it to the King, who ordered it to be put in a cistern full of water, with me in it, as a test. But I could not use my little oars for lack of room.

The Queen had already thought of another project. She ordered the carpenter to make a wooden trough three hundred feet long, fifty feet wide and eight feet deep. Well-coated with tar to prevent leaking, it was placed on the floor, along a wall, in an outer room of the Palace. It had a tap near the bottom, to let water out when it began to get stale, and two servants could easily fill it in half an hour. Here I often used to row to amuse myself as well as the Queen and her ladies, who were entertained by my skill and agility. Sometimes I would put up my sail, and then I only had to steer, while the ladies gave me a wind with their fans. When they were weary, some of the servants would blow my sail forward with their breath, while I showed my skill at steering right-handed or left-handed as I pleased. When I was done, Glumdalclitch always carried my boat to her closet and hung it on a nail to dry.

In this exercise I once had an accident that almost cost me my life. One of the servants had put my boat into the trough. The governess who cared for Glumdalclitch very kindly lifted me up to place me in the boat, but I slipped through her fingers and would have fallen forty feet to the floor, if I had not, by the best luck in the world, been stopped by a pin that stuck in the good woman's gown. The head of the pin passed between my shirt and the waistband of my pants and so I was held by the middle in the air, until Glumdalclitch ran to my relief.

Another time, one of the servants, whose duty it was to fill my trough every third day with fresh water, was so careless that he let a huge frog (that he did not see) slip out of his pail. The frog hid until I was put in my

I BANGED IT A GOOD WHILE WITH ONE OF MY OARS
AND AT LAST FORCED IT TO LEAP OUT OF THE BOAT.

boat, but then, seeing a resting place, he climbed up. He
made the boat lean so much on one side that I was forced

to balance it with all my weight on the other side to prevent it from overturning. When the frog got in, it hopped half the length of the boat and then over my head, backwards and forwards, smearing my face and clothes with its smelly slime. Its large features made it appear the most deformed animal ever born. I wanted Glumdalclitch to let me deal with it alone. I banged it a good while with one of my oars and at last forced it to leap out of the boat.

But the greatest danger I ever faced in that kingdom was from a monkey, who belonged to one of the clerks in the kitchen. Glumdalclitch had locked me up in her room while she went somewhere on a visit. The weather being very warm, the window was left open, as well as the windows and door of my big box, in which I usually lived because of its largeness. As I sat quietly thinking at my table, I heard something bounce in at the window and skip around from one side to another. Although I was very alarmed, I still looked out. Then I saw this playful animal, frisking and leaping up and down. At last he came to my box and peeped in at the door and every window.

I retreated to the corner of my box. But the mon-

REACHING ONE OF HIS PAWS IN AT THE DOOR,
AS A CAT DOES WHEN SHE PLAYS WITH A MOUSE,
HE AT LAST GRABBED MY COAT AND DRAGGED ME OUT.

key, looking in from every side, put me in such a fright
that I did not think to hide under my bed, as I might eas-

ily have done. After some time spent peeping, grinning and chattering, he spied me. Reaching one of his paws in at the door, as a cat does when she plays with a mouse, although I often shifted to avoid him, he at last grabbed my coat and dragged me out.

He took me in his right front paw and held me in his arm as a mother holds her child. When I tried to struggle, he squeezed me so hard that I thought it would be more wise to give in. I believe he took me for a young monkey. He often stroked my face very gently with his other paw. As he was doing this there was a noise at the door, as if somebody were opening it. He suddenly leaped up to the window and from there to a gutter pipe, walking on three legs and holding me with the fourth, until he climbed up on the roof. I heard Glumdalclitch give a shriek at the moment he was carrying me out. The poor girl was almost out of her mind. That quarter of the Palace was all in an uproar. The servants ran for ladders.

The monkey was seen by hundreds in the court, sitting on the ridge of the building, holding me like a baby in one of his front paws. He was feeding me with the other one, cramming into my mouth some food he had squeezed out of a bag he was carrying, patting me when I would not eat. Many in the crowd below could not help laughing. The sight was ridiculous to everybody but myself. Some of the people threw stones, hoping to drive the monkey down, but this was forbidden or else my brains would probably have been knocked out.

The ladders were now put up and mounted by several men. The monkey, seeing that he was almost surrounded and not being able to make speed enough on three legs, let me drop and made his escape. I sat there for some time, five hundred yards from the ground, expecting to be blown down by the wind or to fall from giddiness. But an honest lad, one of my nurse's servants, climbed up, put me in his pants pocket and brought me down safe.

I was almost choked with the filthy stuff the monkey had crammed down my throat. My dear little nurse picked it out of my mouth with a small needle and then I began vomiting, which made me feel better. But I was so weak and bruised from squeezes that I was forced to stay in bed a **fortnight**. The King and Queen asked about my health every day and her Majesty made several visits during my sickness. The monkey was killed and an order issued that no

FORTNIGHT
Two weeks.

such animal should be kept in the Palace.

When I visited the King after my recovery, to thank him for his favors to me, he teased me a good deal about the adventure. He asked me what my thoughts were while I was in the monkey's paw, how I liked the food he gave me, his way of feeding me, and whether the fresh air on the roof had sharpened my appetite. He asked me what I would have done had this happened in my own country. I told his Majesty that in Europe we had no monkeys, except those brought from other parts of the world, and they were so small I could deal with a dozen at once, if they dared to attack me. As for the monster that seized me (it was indeed as large as an elephant), if my fear had allowed me to think of it, I would have used my sword (as I said this I looked fierce and gripped the hilt) when he poked his paw in my box, and given him such a wound that he would have gladly taken it out. I said this in a firm tone, like a person who does not want his courage questioned. However, my speech caused nothing but loud laughter, which the King could not contain.

Every day I supplied the court with some ridiculous story, and Glumdalclitch, though she loved me

dearly, was mischievous enough to tell the Queen when-
ever I committed any folly that she thought might amuse
her Majesty. The girl, who had not been feeling well, was
carried by her governess about thirty miles from town, to
take the air. Glumdalclitch set down my traveling box
near a small footpath in a field, and I went out of it to
walk. There was cow dung in the path and I tried to leap
over it. I took a run, but unfortunately I jumped short
and found myself in the middle up to my knees. I waded
on through and one of the servants wiped me as clean as
he could with his handkerchief. But I was filthy and my
nurse kept me in my box until we were home. The Queen
was soon told what happened, and the servants spread it
around the court, so for some days all the jokes were at
my expense.

Gulliver Shows His Skill at Music and Answers the King's Questions About England

THE KING, WHO DELIGHTED IN MUSIC, HAD frequent concerts at court, to which I was sometimes carried. But the noise was so great that I could hardly make out the tunes. I am confident that all the drums and trumpets of a royal army, beating and sounding together right at your ears, could not equal it. I would have my box moved from places near where the performers sat, as far as I could, then shut the door and windows and draw the curtains, after which I found their music not unpleasant.

I had learned in my youth to play a little on the piano. Glumdalclitch kept one in her room and a master came twice a week to teach her. I call it a piano because it looked like that instrument and was played in the same way. A notion came in my head that I would entertain the King and Queen with an English tune on this instrument. But this appeared extremely difficult. The piano was sixty feet long and each key was a foot wide. With my arms outstretched, I could not reach more than five keys, and to press them down took a good smart stroke with my fist, which would be too much work. The method I thought of was this. I prepared two clubs and covered the thicker ends with pieces of a mouse's skin so they would not damage the keys or make noise. In front of the piano, a bench was placed about four feet below the keys, and I was put on it. I ran along it that way and this, as fast as I could, banging the proper keys with my clubs, and managed to play a jig to the satisfaction of both their Majesties. It was the most violent exercise I ever did. Yet I could not strike more than sixteen keys, or play the bass, which was a great disadvantage to my performance.

The King would often order that I be brought to a table in his room. He would command me to bring a chair out of my box and then sit, which brought me almost to a level with his face. In this manner I had several conversations with him.

One day I took the freedom to tell his Majesty that the power of reason is not equal to the size of the body. Among animals, bees and ants have reputations for being more hardworking, skillful and wise than many larger animals. And, as small as he took me to be, I still hoped to do his Majesty some important service. The King listened to me with attention and began to have a better opinion of me. He asked me to tell him about the government of England so that he could learn of things he might also do.

I wished I had the tongue of **Cicero** to celebrate my dear country in the style it deserves. I dwelt on our soil and climate. I spoke about our Parliament and the education of our nobles to be advisors to the King and champions

CICERO
The greatest of the Roman orators.

HE WOULD COMMAND ME TO BRING A CHAIR OUT OF MY BOX AND
THEN SIT, WHICH BROUGHT ME ALMOST TO A LEVEL WITH HIS FACE.

ready to defend him. I told of our bishops, who take care of religion, and who are the spiritual fathers of the people. I described our courts and judges, wise men who decide the rights of men, punish wickedness and protect the innocent. I mentioned the management of our treasury and the bravery of our forces on land and sea. I did not forget our sports or anything that was to the honor of my country, and I finished with a brief history of England in the last hundred years.

This conversation continued over five meetings, each several hours long, and the King heard all with attention. When I was at an end, his Majesty, looking over his notes, raised many doubts and questions. He asked what qualifications were necessary to be a noble and whether they were free from bribes. He asked how much time was spent judging between right and wrong and at what cost. He asked about our taxes and, noting our many wars, if we were quarrelsome, or lived among very bad neighbors. He was amazed to hear that we, as free people, have an army during times of peace. He said our history was only a heap of conspiracies, murders and massacres, the worst that greed, hatred, envy and cruelty could make.

Then, taking me in his hand and stroking me gently, he said these words, which I shall never forget, "My little friend Grildrig, by what I have gathered from your story, and the answers I have wrung from you, I conclude your people are the most evil pests that nature ever let crawl on the surface of the earth."

It was pointless for me to resent these words. I was forced to rest with patience while my noble and beloved country was so injured. But great allowance must be given to a king who lives entirely cut off from the rest of the world and is unfamiliar with the customs of other nations. Lack of knowledge always causes many prejudices and narrow thinking. It would be hard indeed, if such a king's notions of right and wrong were held up as a standard for mankind.

To show the results of a limited education, I shall tell what happened when I made a proposal to his Majesty that was greatly to his advantage. In hopes of getting his favor, I told him of the invention and uses of gunpowder. "A proper quantity of this powder," I said, "rammed into a hollow tube of brass or iron, can drive a ball of lead with such violence and speed that nothing can withstand its force. The largest balls can destroy whole ranks of an army at once, batter the strongest walls to the ground, sink ships with a thousand men in them to the bottom of the sea, and if joined together with chains, can cut through masts, slice hundreds of bodies through the middle, and lay waste to everything in front of them." I told him we often put this powder inside large iron balls and then fired the balls into cities we were attacking, ripping up pavement, tearing houses to pieces, and throwing metal splinters into all who were near.

I said I knew how to make gunpowder cheaply, and cannons and shells, and could show his workmen. He would have the power to batter down a town in a few hours if it refused one of his commands. I humbly offered this knowledge to his Majesty.

The King was horrified at the description and the proposal I made. He was amazed that a helpless, groveling insect (that was his phrase) such as I could think such inhuman ideas and appear unmoved at the scenes of blood and ruin I painted. He said an evil genius, an enemy of mankind, must have first made such machines. As for himself, though few things delighted him more than a discovery in art or nature, he said he would rather lose half his kingdom than know such a secret. He commanded me, as I valued my life, never to mention it anymore.

This is the strange result of narrow principles and short views! This king, who possessed every quality that wins admiration, love and respect, who was wise and well-educated, who was adored by his people, let slip from his hands the power to be the absolute master of their lives, liberties and fortunes. I do not say this to speak ill of that excellent King. His flaw rose from ignorance, from not seeing politics as a science, as do the more brilliant men in Europe.

I remember very well one day with the King when I happened to say that in England we have a thousand books on the art of government. It gave him a bad opinion of us. He said he hated all secrecy and treachery in a prince or minister. He said the knowledge of governing amounted to common sense and reason, to justice and mercy, and to speedy judgments in the law courts. His opinion was that whoever could make two ears of corn, or two blades of grass, grow on the same spot where only one had grown before did more for his country than all the politicians put together.

The learning of his people is very lacking. They

I CLIMBED TO THE TOP STEP OF THE LADDER, FACED THE BOOK,
AND WALKED TO THE RIGHT ABOUT EIGHT OR TEN PACES,
DEPENDING ON THE LENGTH OF THE LINES.

know only morality, history, poetry and mathematics, although it must be admitted, in these they excel. But
mathematics is applied only to what is useful in life, such
as improving farming or manufacturing.

No laws in their country can have more words than there are letters in their alphabet, which amount to two and twenty. Indeed, few of them are even that long. They are expressed in the most plain and simple terms, so there is only one meaning.

They have had the art of printing, just like the Chinese, for a very long time. But their libraries are not very large. The King's, which is the largest, has no more than a thousand volumes. I was at liberty to borrow books as I pleased. The Queen's carpenter made a kind of wooden ladder twenty-five feet high, each step of which was fifty feet wide. It was a moveable set of stairs. The book I wanted to read was put up leaning against the wall. I climbed to the top step of the ladder, faced the book, and walked to the right about eight or ten paces, depending on the length of the lines. And so I descended gradually until I got to the bottom of the page, and then I started over again. I could easily turn a page with both hands, for they were as thick and stiff as cardboard.

Their style of writing is clear and smooth. They avoid unnecessary words and using expressions. I read many of their books, especially in history and morality. I was very taken with a little old book which always lay in

A CAVALIER ON A STEED MIGHT BE NINETY FEET HIGH.

Glumdalclitch's bedroom and belonged to her governess, a serious, elderly woman who preferred to read about spiritual matters. The book deals with the weakness of humankind and is generally read only by women and common people.

They boast of their army, if it can be called that. It is made up of tradesmen from the cities and farmers from the country, whose commanders are nobles, chosen by ballot. I have often seen the militia of Lorbrulgrud exercise in a field near the city. A cavalier on a steed might be ninety feet high. I have seen this cavalry draw their swords at once and wave them in the air. Nothing is so grand, so surprising and so astonishing. It looked as if ten thousand lightning flashes were darting from the sky.

I was curious to know how this King, whose lands cannot be reached from any other country, came to think of armies. I was told, and learned from reading their histories, that over the ages they have been troubled by the same disease to which we are subject. The nobles seek power, the people seek liberty, the kings seek absolute rule, and civil wars result.

CHAPTER 7

Gulliver Returns to England

I ALWAYS HAD A STRONG FEELING THAT I WOULD some time recover my liberty, but it was impossible to imagine how it might happen. The ship in which I sailed was the first ever seen from that coast, and the King had given orders that if another appeared, it should be taken and all its crew and passengers brought to Lorbrulgrud. He strongly wished to get a woman of my size, so that we might have children. But I would rather die than leave descendants to be kept in cages like canaries, and perhaps even sold as curiosities.

I was indeed treated with kindness. I was a favorite of the King and Queen and the whole court, but it was under conditions that did not suit human dignity. I wanted to be among people I could talk to on even terms, and walk the streets without fear of being crushed to death like a frog or a puppy.

I had now been in this country two years and, about the beginning of the third, Glumdalclitch and I went with the King and Queen on a tour of the south coast of the kingdom. I was carried as usual in my traveling box. I had ordered a hammock fixed by silk ropes to the four corners of the top, to break the jolts when a servant carried me on horseback. I would often sleep in my hammock while we were on the road. I had the carpenter cut a hole a foot square on the roof of my box to give me air. I could shut the hole with a board that drew back and forth in a groove.

When we came to our destination, the King chose to pass a few days at a palace he had near Flanflasnic, a city about eighteen miles from the sea. Glumdalclitch and I were very tired. I had a small cold, but the poor girl was so ill she had to stay in her room. I longed to see the ocean, which must be my only route of escape, if ever it should happen. I pretended to be worse than I really was and asked permission to take the fresh air of the sea with a servant who was sometimes trusted with me.

I shall never forget the unwillingness with which Glumdalclitch agreed, nor the strict instructions she gave to the servant to be careful with me. At the same time, she burst into a flood of tears, as if she had some foreboding of what was going to happen. The boy took me out of my box about a half-hour's walk from the palace, towards the rocks on the seashore. I ordered him to set me down and, lifting one of my sashes, I looked sadly towards the sea. I felt ill and told the servant I had a mind to take a nap in my hammock. He shut the window, to keep out the cold, and I soon fell asleep.

All I can suppose is that while I slept, the servant, thinking no danger could happen, went looking for bird eggs among the rocks. Earlier, I had seen him searching and picking up one or two in the clefts. In any case, I found myself suddenly awakened with a violent pull on the handle on the top of my box. I felt the box raised very high in the air and then carried forward with amazing speed. The first jolt almost shook me out of my

hammock, but after that the motion was easy enough. I
called out several times as loud as I could, but to no purpose. I looked out the windows but could see nothing
but clouds and sky. I heard a noise over my head like the
flapping of wings, and then I began to realize that some
eagle had got the ring of my box in his beak, intending
to let it fall on a rock, like a turtle in a shell, and then pick
out my body and eat it.

In a little time I noticed the noise and flutter of
wings increase very fast and my box was tossed up and
down like a sign on a windy day. I heard several blows
given to the eagle, or so I thought, and then, all of a sudden, I felt myself falling straight down for more than a
minute. The drop was so fast I almost lost my breath. My
fall stopped with a terrible splash that sounded to me
like the Niagara Falls. I was in the dark for another
minute and then my box began to rise so that I could see
light at the tops of my windows. I now realized I had fall-
en into the sea. My box floated about five feet deep in the
water. I supposed then, and still do, that the eagle that
flew away with my box was followed by others, and he
was forced to let me drop while he was defending himself
from them, who wanted a share of me. My room was

I HEARD SEVERAL BLOWS GIVEN TO THE EAGLE AND THEN,
ALL OF A SUDDEN, I FELT MYSELF FALLING STRAIGHT
DOWN FOR MORE THAN A MINUTE.

built so tightly that very little water leaked in. Once I
managed to get out of my hammock, I drew back the
board in my roof to let in air.

How often did I wish I was with my dear Glumdalclitch, who in one single hour had been so far separated from me! I can truthfully say, even in the midst of my troubles, I could not help but be sorry for my poor nurse, for the grief she would feel at losing me and at the anger of the Queen. Meanwhile, I expected at every moment to see my box dashed to pieces or overturned by the first violent wind or a rising wave. A break in a single piece of glass would have been immediate death. Water oozed in several places, but the leaks were not large. I could not lift the roof of my room, otherwise I would have sat on the top. But even if I escaped danger for a day or two, what could I expect but a miserable death from cold and hunger!

I have already mentioned the two strong staples on my box that servants would buckle their leather belts to. After four hours in my despairing state, I heard, or thought I heard, a grating noise on the side of my box where the staples were. Soon I began to think the box was being pulled, or towed along. Now and then, I felt tugging that made waves rise nearly above my windows and left me almost in the dark. This gave me some faint hope of being saved.

I unscrewed one of my chairs, put it directly under the slipping board, climbed on it, and called for help in a loud voice and in all the languages I knew. Then I fastened my handkerchief to a walking stick I usually carried and, thrusting it through the hole, waved it in the air so that if any ship were near, the sailors might think some unhappy man was shut up in the box.

I found nothing happened from anything I did, but after an hour the box struck something hard. I feared it was a rock. I plainly heard a noise outside my roof and then felt myself hoisted up at least three feet higher than I was before. So I thrust up my handkerchief again and called for help until I was hoarse.

In return I heard a great shout, repeated three times, which gave me such joy it cannot be imagined except by someone who has felt it. Now I heard trampling over my head and someone called down though the hole in the English tongue, "If there be anybody below, let them speak."

I answered I was an Englishman, drawn by bad luck into the greatest disaster any creature ever survived. I begged to be delivered from the dungeon I was in.

The voice said I was safe and that the carpenter would come and cut a hole in the cover to get me out. That was needless and would take too much time, I said. Just let a crewman put his finger through the ring and take the box up to the captain's cabin. Hearing me talk so wildly, some of them thought I was mad. Others laughed. Indeed, it never came into my head that I was among people of my own size and strength. The carpenter came, and in a few minutes I was taken onto the ship in a very weak condition.

The sailors were all amazed and asked me a thousand questions that I did not feel like answering. I thought they were **pygmies**, because my eyes were so used to enormous objects. The captain, Mr. Thomas Wilcocks, an honest **Shropshire** man, seeing I was ready to faint, took me to his cabin, gave me brandy, and put me in his own bed.

PYGMIES
A people of the African rain forests famous for their small size.

SHROPSHIRE
An English county bordering Wales.

Before I went to sleep I told the captain I had some valuable furniture in my box too good to be lost. He sent men down into my room. They brought up all my goods, stripped off the quilting, and tore off some boards for the use of the ship. When

I WAS TAKEN ONTO THE SHIP IN A VERY WEAK CONDITION.

they got all they had a mind for, they let the hulk drop into the sea. I was glad not to see it happen, because I am sure it would have touched me and brought memories to mind I would rather forget.

I slept some hours, but was constantly disturbed by dreams of the place I had left and the dangers I had escaped. Upon waking I felt much better. The captain entertained me with great kindness and asked me to tell him the story of my travels and how I came to be set adrift in that huge wooden chest. He said that at about noon, he spied my box through his glass and sent a long-boat out to discover what it was. His men came back in a fright, swearing they had seen a swimming house. He laughed at them and went himself in the boat. He rowed around me several times, noticing the windows and their wire screens, and at last fastened a cable to one of the staples, ordering his men to tow my chest (as he called it) to the ship.

I asked if he saw any enormous birds about the time he discovered me. He answered that a sailor had seen three eagles flying toward the north, but they were not bigger than usual. I suppose that must be because of the great height they were at.

I then asked how far we might be from land. He said at least a hundred leagues. I assured him he must be mistaken because I had only been two hours away from the country I was in when I dropped into the sea. At that, he began to think again that my brain was disturbed and he advised me to go back to bed. I assured him I felt well-refreshed. Then he grew serious and asked if I was troubled in my mind with a crime I had committed, for which I was punished by being cast away in the chest. He said his suspicions were raised by my absurd speeches, as well as my odd behavior.

I begged him to hear my story, which I faithfully told from the last time I left England until he discovered me. The truth always forces its way into reasonable minds. So this honest gentleman, who had a trace of learning, was convinced of my truthfulness. But, to prove what I said, I asked for my cabinet to be brought. I opened it in his presence and showed him the rare things I had collected. There was a comb made from the stumps of the King's beard, some combings of the Queen's hair, four wasp stingers, a gold ring the Queen one day took from her little finger and gave me to wear like a collar, and the pants I had on, made from a mouse's skin. Nothing was

NOTHING WAS CURIOUS TO HIM BUT A SERVANT'S TOOTH,
WHICH A SURGEON HAD PULLED BY MISTAKE.

curious to him but a servant's tooth, which a surgeon had
pulled by mistake from one of Glumdalclitch's men. It was
about a foot long and four inches wide.

The captain was satisfied with my story and said he hoped, when we returned to England, that I would put it on paper and make it public. I said nothing in it would pass for extraordinary compared to what other authors wrote.

He said he wondered one thing, which was, hearing me speak so loud, if the people of that country were thick of hearing. I told him his men seemed to speak in only a whisper, yet I could hear them. But, in that country, it was as if I was a man on the street talking to a man who was on a steeple, unless I was held in his hand. I had gotten used to the huge size of things and winked at my littleness, as people do at their own faults.

Our voyage to England was prosperous. We landed on the 3rd of June, 1706, nine months after my escape. I made the captain promise to come see me at my house in Redriff and hired a horse. While I was on the road, observing the littleness of people and houses, the trees and cattle, I began to think I was in Lilliput. I was afraid of trampling travelers I met and yelled at them to stand out of the way. I almost got my head broken once or twice for my rudeness.

MY WIFE RAN OUT TO EMBRACE ME, BUT I STOOPED
LOWER THAN HER KNEES, THINKING SHE COULD OTHERWISE
NEVER BE ABLE TO REACH MY MOUTH.

When I came to my own house, which I was
forced to ask directions to find, I bent down to go in (like
a goose going under a gate) for fear of striking my head.

My wife ran out to embrace me, but I stooped lower than her knees, thinking she could otherwise never be able to reach my mouth. My daughter kneeled to ask my blessing, but I could not see her until she stood up, having been so long used to looking above sixty feet in the air. In short, I behaved so strangely they believed I had lost my wits. I mention this as an example of the great power of habit and prejudice.

In a little time, my family and I came to a right understanding, but my wife protested I should never go to sea anymore. In the meantime, here I end my story.

Jonathan Swift

1 6 6 7 - 1 7 4 5

JONATHAN SWIFT WAS BORN IN DUBLIN, IRELAND, a few months after his father died. His parents were English. When he was little, his mother returned to England and left him in Ireland with his uncle, who later sent him to Trinity College in Dublin. He was an independent-minded student, but he earned his degree and later became a minister in the Church of Ireland.

As a young man, he went to England to work for a retired diplomat who once introduced him to King William III. Swift and the King walked together through a garden and the King showed Swift how to cut asparagus. Swift later ventured to offer the King political advice, but the King rejected it. Swift said that reminded him not to think of himself as too important.

He wrote many political essays, first in support of liberal ideas and later on the side of conservatives, whose views were closer to those of the church. Swift wanted to be a bishop, but because some of his opinions were unpopular in the church, he never reached that rank. He did become the head of St. Patrick's Cathedral in Dublin.

Swift wrote essays against the harsh British treatment of the Irish, and these made him a hero to the Irish people. In a famous essay titled "A Modest Proposal," he pretended to be serious about saying that the problems in Ireland could be solved by eating the babies of poor people. He was always ready to use strong words to express his outrage over brutality and injustice.

He wrote *Gulliver's Travels*, his most famous book, when he was almost 60 years old. It was instantly popular. One of his London friends wrote to tell him that it was being read everywhere, from the King's council to children's nurseries. Swift is still admired for having a clear, forceful style of writing that is a model of good English.

In old age, he suffered from an ear disease that sometimes made him deaf and unable to stand up. When he died, he left money to build a hospital for the insane.